Books

by

Paul W. Feenstra

Published by Mellester Press.

Boundary

The Breath of God (Book 1 in Moana Rangitira series)

For Want of a Shilling (Book 2 in Moana Rangitira series)

Falls Ende
eBook series
Falls Ende – The Oath (eBook 1)
Falls Ende – Courser   (eBook 2)
Falls Ende – The King (eBook 3)

Falls Ende – Primus (Print version of eBook compilation 1, 2 & 3)Book 1

Falls Ende – Secundus   Book 2

Falls Ende – Tertium   Book 3

Gunpowder Green

Gunpowder Green

Published in New Zealand
A catalogue record of this book is available from
the National Library of New Zealand.
Kei te pātengi raraunga o Te Puna Mātauranga o
Aotearoa te whakarārangi o tēnei pukapuka

With heartfelt thanks.

Cover Design, Mea
Edited by Hannah Ross

http://www.paulwfeenstra.com/
Gunpowder Green © 2021 Mellester Press

Gunpowder Green ISBN 978-0-473-57401-7 Softcover
Gunpowder Green ISBN 978-0-473-57402-4 hardcover
Gunpowder Green ISBN 978-0-473-57403-1 epub
Gunpowder Green ISBN 978-0-473-57404-8 Kindle
Gunpowder Green ISBN 978-0-473-57405-5 iBook

Published by

Mellester Press

GUNPOWDER GREEN

by

Paul W. Feenstra

A nostalgic and colourful collection
of rural New Zealand short-stories

It's been suggested that a young English clerk thought the tiny pellets of a Chinese green tea looked like gunpowder and coined the name 'Gunpowder Green'. However, it is also likely the name originated from Mandarin Chinese. A variation on the phrase for, 'freshly brewed', is *'gāng pào de'*.

Gunpowder Green

Table of Contents

GUNPOWDER GREEN

Chapter One

Taranaki, 1885

Burt Jenkins was a man of habit, staunch in his belief that if something worked the first time, one should apply the same process thereafter, and with such a mindset, he went about making his morning brew exactly as he did every day. He carefully measured three spoons of tiny tea pellets, removed the pot of boiling water from the stove, mumbled, "one for the pot and two for me," and poured the bubbling water into his old silver teapot. He placed the dented lid securely on top and, while he waited for the tea to draw, thought about the day ahead.

Exactly four minutes later he rotated the teapot twice, in a clockwise motion and not too vigorously, then poured the steaming brew, through a strainer, and into a chipped bone China cup. Holding the cup delicately in his thick, stubby fingers, he went out to the deck and turned west. Bathed in the soft golden light of dawn, Mount Egmont proudly looked down over fertile Taranaki farmlands and abundant green bush. The view was breathtaking and a sight he never tired of. He breathed in the cool morning air and surveyed the majestic panoramic view while he sipped his brew with pleasure. Clouds were forming on the mountain's eastern side and he knew it would rain later that morning.

Burt's hundred-acre farm lay about forty miles east from Mount Egmont and nestled in rugged, steep, bush-covered hill country. Not much good for cows, and any land he cleared of native bush, he grazed with sheep and a few goats. Additionally, he leased five acres of prime flat land from old man Brooks, a friendly neighbour, for his beef cattle. Sadly, Tim Brooks passed away recently and his holdings were sold. Many locals speculated that Tim's excessive drinking finally caught up to him and his liver packed up - this irritated Burt, who detested idle gossip. Burt knew full well that Tim suffered from an ailing heart, and that was what killed him. A new owner moved onto Tim's property yesterday and Burt decided to pay a visit, introduce himself, and bring a batch of scones he baked two nights ago as a welcome gift.

With no wife, Burt did all his own cooking and baking, and when needed, even a spot of cleaning once in a while. It was a good life; he was content and happy and didn't miss female company at all.

Although he was married once, it was a long time ago. His wife had been lazy and talked far too much and, to his delight, took off with a sheep drover from Ohakune. He never missed her and hoped the poor fella wasn't mad at him for not asking her to come back. Living alone suited Burt. He had his dog, horse, sheep, cows, goats and, of course, an obnoxious old billy to keep him occupied.

With a dozen scones wrapped in muslin cloth and buried safely in a satchel, Burt set off on horseback to visit the new owners of the nearby farm. As he accurately predicted, the weather had changed. It was now overcast, and he hoped the rain would hold off until after he returned home.

To ward off the chilly wind, he turned his collar up and secured his oilskin hat as he navigated the treacherous path down onto the flat Taranaki plains. After a while, he turned onto a long, rutted track that would take him to his new neighbour.

Burt was impressed. Grazing in a paddock were two healthy and very expensive Clydesdale draught horses. When Tim Brooks passed away all his livestock was sold, and the new owners had transported their own animals to the extensive farm before they'd moved in. He saw a sizeable herd of cattle, and in another paddock, a massive bull. His keen farmer's eye missed nothing, not even the herd of impressive Angora goats that nibbled at the native trees at the border fence line of his property. "The bloke's got some money, that's for sure," he said aloud to no one in particular.

His first encounter with the new owners was slightly less impressive. As he approached the homestead, two boys playing outside quickly ran away yelling, "Dad, an old man is coming!"

While certainly not a young man anymore, Burt was rather put out. He'd never thought of himself as *old* but, giving the boys the benefit of the doubt, he cast aside his negative thoughts and proceeded to Tim's old house, dismounted, and tethered his horse to a rail.

"Mornin'," came the voice of a youngish man. His broad smile was welcoming and genuine.

"G'day," Burt returned the greeting. "I'm Burt Jenkins, your neighbour from up the hill." Burt waved behind him in the general direction of Mount Ruapehu, which lay somewhere to the northeast, and then extended a calloused hand.

"Pleasure to meet ya, Mr. Jenkins. I'm Thomas Warner." He returned the gesture and they shook.

"Ya bought yourself a beaut property. Good land, this, good for farming, Tom," said Burt with a big smile of his own.

"I'm sure we'll be happy here," replied Mr. Warner. "Would you like to come in and have a cup of tea?"

"Thought you'd never ask," replied Burt as he retrieved his scones from the satchel. "Scones. Made 'em m'self. A welcome present for the family."

"You are most kind, Mr. Jenkins. Come and you can meet the boys and Maggie. She's inside."

Mr. Warner and Burt climbed the steps to the veranda that wrapped around the entire house. "Lovely home, isn't it?" added Burt as they approached the door.

"Oh yes, we are very pleased with it. Have you been here before, Mr. Jenkins?"

"Many times. Me and ol' Tim were good mates and I came here often. And, uh, please call me Burt, everyone else does."

The large door swung open and the space was immediately filled by a rather hefty woman. She reminded Burt of one of the cows in the paddock he passed on the way up.

The woman gave Burt a quick look from head to toe. He was about to introduce himself to her when she spoke first. "You ain't comin' in here with them boots on, are ya?"

"I, uh, I was… nope," he replied.

"Maggie, this is Burt Jenkins, our neighbor up the hill," explained Mr. Warner, ignoring her comment. "He's come to welcome us. He even brought some scones as a gift. I thought we could have a cuppa and chat."

"Lovely to meet you, Maggie." Burt removed his hat and dipped his head, giving her his best and warmest smile.

"Mrs. Warner, please," she corrected. "Ah, so you are a local, eh? We've heard some rather unsavory things, you know," she frowned. "But now as you are here, I suppose you'd better come in. Boots off." She glowered at him with arms folded. She did not move her bulk from the doorway and stared, challenging him to defy her.

A couple of unopened crates of possessions cluttered the floor of their spacious kitchen, but a table and chairs had been conveniently positioned near tall bay windows that overlooked a lush green paddock. In the distance, Burt could see the pure white Angora goats still tugging at his native trees.

"Does Gunpowder Green suit you, Mr. Jenkins?" Mr. Warner said, looking over his shoulder as he stoked the fire in the stove.

Mrs. Warner was sighing loudly as she reluctantly arranged cups and saucers.

Burt raised his eyebrows and smiled. "Ah, Gunpowder Green, my favourite. If it's no problem, Tom. Thank you."

"I don't think so," snapped Mrs. Warner. "We'll have Earl Grey. You know we keep the Gunpowder Green for important occasions, Thomas."

"Yes, of course, dear," Mr. Warner replied dutifully as he put the water on to boil.

Dismayed, Burt looked down at the floor. He saw his big toe sticking through a hole in his sock and was reminded he needed to do some darning.

Burt's scones sat heaped on a plate in the centre of the table. His own tea, now cold, was also largely untouched. He wasn't fussed with Earl Grey.

Mr. and Mrs. Warner's two sons came running through the house. "Say hello to Mr. Jenkins, boys," Mr. Warner smiled proudly and then pointed: "This is Peter and this is young William."

"Nice to meet ya," offered Burt, nodding to each boy.

"We want a scone, Mum," demanded the oldest, showing no interest in their guest. The younger had a finger buried in his nose and stared up at the ceiling. Burt looked up as well. It turned out there was nothing to see.

"Absolutely not," barked Mrs. Warner. "Outside, both of you."

All twelve scones remained untouched as the two darlings ran from the room.

"Maggie has a passion for Angora goats. You may have seen them when you rode up. Is kind of her hobby," volunteered Mr. Warner.

"It's not a hobby, it's a business and an extra source of income," she bit back with a scowl.

Burt determined that Maggie wasn't having a good day. "Oh, is that right? Yep, saw them. Fine looking goats," he added.

"They're not just any ordinary old goat. They're Angoras, prized for their mohair. Grows very fast," she said, raising her eyebrows.

"How lovely," Burt replied.

"She adores them and is hoping to breed," said Mr. Warner. "We can't wait to have Angora kids frolicking in the paddock. Heaven forbid anything happens to her precious white goats... they get more attention than I do." He gave his wife a coy smile and laughed.

She didn't return the smile or laugh, but just stared coldly.

Burt believed Tom and thought there was an element of truth to his last statement. He saw the first drops of rain hit the window. He wanted to leave. "Well, as much as I'd love to stay and chat, the weather's turn'n and I've got work to do." He eased himself upright.

"Oh, before you go, Mr. Jenkins," said Mrs. Warner, "we have a small herd of under-nourished and neglected beef cattle on a small parcel of our property. We were informed by our stock agent that the land is leased to a local and were told the owner is a hard-case and a bit of a troublemaker. By any chance, you wouldn't know who he is, would you?"

Burt scratched the back of his head and gave the question due consideration. "Under-nourished...? Troublemaker, eh? Nah, can't help you there, Maggie. Sorry. Don't know who that would be. A shame to have, uh, neglected animals on your property, isn't it?"

"Worms."

"Pardon me?" Burt asked.

"Got gut worms, and please, call me Mrs. Warner."

"Oh, I hope you get rid of them soon – Maggie," Burt remarked innocently. "I understand it's a bit rough on the stomach."

"Not me," she growled. "Those cows on our land probably have worms."

Burt smiled and nodded. "Of course, more'n likely. Thank you very much for your kind hospitality, but I really must be off."

Chapter Two

The snow-capped volcano, Mount Egmont, was awash in a soft, pink early morning light. On the flats below, he could see small pockets of mist, while higher, on the far side of Egmont's peak, clouds gathered. He doubted it would rain. Perhaps tonight, but not today. He lifted the cup to his mouth and swallowed the last mouthful of tea. Time to go to work.

With his bullock pulling the wagon loaded with tools, and his dog gleefully off the chain and running ahead, Burt set off down the track to clear scrub and bush to make way for more pasture for his sheep. It was an endless but rewarding job, and he didn't mind the hard work at all.

In preparation for clearing the bush, Burt had allowed his goats in ahead of time. They ate anything and everything and with them wandering around, they created paths through the scrub, making access on the steep slopes easier for him. He deliberately kept a green belt of native trees that provided shelter along his border, while a wooden-rail fence kept his own goats away from the very same trees that the Warners' Angora goats had been eating. He wasn't amused.

His own billy goat was a disagreeable animal. It stunk and was unafraid of humans and dogs. It was a pest and pretty much did as it pleased. He'd thought many a day that the animal would be better served as dog tucker, but due to his kind nature, held off slaughtering it. He believed the old billy goat would die of natural causes soon enough.

Once he reached the lower slopes of his property, he immediately looked for the billy. The nannies were where he expected them to be, but of the billy goat there was no sign. He began searching and soon found where the animal had broken through his border fence. With horror, he saw it amid Maggie's much-loved Angoras. Guiltily, he looked down at the Warners' house and luckily saw no activity down there. He hoped they didn't notice as the thought of confronting Maggie about his wayward billy left a foul taste in his mouth. He shuddered. Perhaps now was the time to put the old billy out of his misery, he thought. His carbine was back in the wagon.

The billy stood, curiously facing him, while the skittish Angora nannies moved away and kept their distance. In most respects, his billy goat was unremarkable and just partially domesticated which, according to Burt, meant the beast was half wild. Its chest and neck were black and its back and rear legs were tan. Like its face, the lower front legs beneath its knees were white, as if it wore socks. Burt had removed its horns a couple of years ago, but it still had hard nubs that hurt when it put its head down and butted him.

Burt was ready and bravely enticed the goat to charge. As soon as it made its move, he would quickly step back across the fence and hope the billy would follow. The billy didn't move, however, and just watched him with only mild interest. Burt edged a step closer, but it just stood looking stupidly, its jaw in constant motion as it chewed on something. Burt risked another quick look at the Warners' house. Thankfully, no one was outside.

As soon as Burt looked away, the billy stopped chewing and charged.

It lowered its head and sprung forward, directly at him. If he didn't move quickly, he'd have a painful bruise on his hip or thigh and limp around for a day or two, so he had no intention of allowing the goat to hurt him. Burt turned, leapt over the fence, and waited. The billy's smell was nauseating. In rutting season, billies urinated over their face and legs to make themselves more attractive to females – and this billy reeked – he was high.

"C'mon, boy, c'mon," encouraged Burt, coaxing the animal to return to the correct side of the fence. "That's it… just a bit more…" The billy leapt across the gap and rushed for him, but a sturdy broken tree branch he held kept the goat at a safe distance. After a moment or two, the old goat lost interest in him and slowly walked back towards his own nannies further up the hill. Thankfully, a crisis was averted and Burt was somewhat relieved.

A closer inspection of the fence revealed what had happened. The Angoras had pushed through a rotten wooden rail and tugged it free, which allowed his billy to escape. Burt returned to the wagon and retrieved a new wooden fence rail, a hammer, and some nails. They wouldn't do that again.

Burt Jenkins didn't receive many visitors; in fact, he couldn't remember the last time anyone had ventured this high into the hills to come and see him. When his dog began barking one overcast afternoon, he looked up and was surprised to see a man riding up the track towards him. As the rider approached, Burt saw it was his new neighbour, Thomas Warner. Burt looked to see if Maggie was following, but quickly surmised it would have been too much effort for her. Tom was alone.

"G'day, Tom, good to see ya. It's been a while."

"Afternoon, Mr. Jenkins. Yep, it has."

"Call me Burt, Tom… is easier, eh? What brings you up here into

Jenkins country? I don't get many visitors up here."

"Yeah, I thought I'd ride up and see ya."

"Let's go inside and have a cuppa, eh? I was going to put the kettle on anyway."

"Thank you, Mr. Jenkins, I'd like that, but I can't be away long. Maggie is expecting me back soon."

"Oh, I'm sure she won't mind," said Burt as he guided Tom to his small cottage. "Gunpowder Green all right with ya? I don't have Earl Grey."

"Oh, well then, in that case, yes, please."

Using his forearm, Burt swept a few bits and pieces from the kitchen table, including a file and a saw blade he was sharpening. A small tin of gun oil fell onto the floor and a couple of dirty plates were put in a bucket, where they would eventually be washed. The tea had been drawing for exactly four minutes, and Burt gently turned the pot twice before pouring two cups and offering his guest a biscuit.

"And to what do I owe the pleasure of your visit, Tom?" asked Burt after taking a sip.

Tom's face clouded over. "Well, uh, Maggie wanted to talk to you about something and she was going to drop a letter in the post asking you to come down and have a friendly chat. I suggested I could ride up to see you and save some time and bother."

"Oh, is that right?" Burt scratched the stubble on his chin. He didn't believe for one moment Maggie wanted to have a *friendly* chat. There was more, of that he was certain. "Any idea what it's about?" He raised an eyebrow.

Tom was staring into his cup and looked awkward.

"Is it important, Tom? Why can't we chat about it now that you're here?"

Tom looked up and placed the cup on the table. "Maggie makes all the decisions," he shrugged. "It's really up to her."

Burt gave a slow nod of understanding. "Alrighty, I'll be down tomorrow if that suits, about ten-ish."

Burt watched Tom ride away and slowly walked back to his house and onto the porch. He looked ahead at where Mount Egmont should be. The volcano was shrouded in clouds and couldn't be seen. An ominous sign.

He couldn't fathom why Maggie wanted to see him. The only possible reason he could think of was that she found out he was the farmer who had leased the land from Tim and most likely wanted an explanation as to why he didn't say so when she'd asked. As a matter of fact, his cows were in prime condition and he'd be taking some of them to the Patea Meat Preserving Company for slaughter soon. Her accusation they were undernourished and neglected was pure nonsense and that irked him. He wasn't concerned. He'd paid Tim Brooks for the lease a year in advance and, by his reckoning, still had about nine months left.

Chapter Three

As he slowly rode down the track of his property, Burt surveyed his land and made mental notes as to what work needed to be done. When he neared the bottom, he paused and looked out at where his sheep grazed on newly cleared slopes. He just wished he had more flat pasture for his cows so he didn't have to lease land from others.

He hated being dependent on another farmer for land, but when the government gave him the block, a reward for serving in the army and fighting in the Māori land wars a few years ago, he had no choice. He'd even gone to Māori Iwi and paid them for the land he occupied, as he believed it was confiscated unfairly. He asked them if they would sell him more, but all prime flat land had been sold or was being used. That was when old Tim offered to lease him some land at a very fair price.

He continued down and then made the turn onto the Warners' property. Automatically, he looked up the fence line for the Angoras but didn't see any of them. *Good*, he thought. *At least they're not chewing on my trees or fence.*

"G'day, Mr. Jenkins," yelled Mr. Warner as he walked out from behind the chicken coop.

"Mornin', Tom, and a lovely day it is," replied Burt as he dismounted.

He tethered his horse to a rail and loosened the saddle as Tom walked up, carrying some eggs.

"Thanks for comin'. Let's go inside, shall we?"

Burt was removing his boots when the door opened and Mrs. Warner darkened the space. She appraised him with her familiar, quick up and down look and then showed her teeth. Burt assumed this was supposed to be a smile and offered her one in return. "Mornin', Maggie, how are ya today?"

Her teeth disappeared. "Mrs. Warner, please, Mr. Jenkins. And I've had better mornings."

"Come in, Mr. Jenkins, and I'll fix a brew, eh?" offered Tom.

Mrs. Warner reluctantly moved aside and shuffled into the kitchen after them.

"You've been busy. We've seen how you cleared all that land at the bottom of the hill," Mr. Warner offered.

"Yep, a lot of work, but I enjoy it and it keeps me out of trouble," laughed Burt.

No one else did.

"Uh, we've been busy too. Since we saw you last, we purchased an Angora billy and built a pen for the goats. It was rutting season a month or two back, and we are now expecting our first kids in about ten weeks," said Tom proudly as he waited for the water to boil. "Gunpowder Green suit ya, Mr. Jenkins?"

He looked at Mrs. Warner, who was choking a tea-towel. "That would be lovely, thanks, Tom."

"We're counting the days and can't wait for the birth of our first Angoras. Maggie wants to be New Zealand's biggest Angora breeder. She's already begun spreading the word and received some down payments from advance orders. Isn't that right, dear?"

Maggie was bent over, putting more wood in the stove. Burt thought she had indeed been spreading.

She grunted in agreement as she slowly straightened and turned to face him. Burt noticed that Mr. Warner didn't make her a cup of tea.

"Mr. Jenkins, I don't appreciate being lied to. I think if we want to keep on social, friendly terms, we should have honesty between us, isn't this so?" she stated coldly.

Burt slowly raised the cup to his mouth and sipped noisily. *It isn't a bad cuppa, but Tom could have let it draw a little longer.* Careful not to spill any tea, he placed the cup back on the saucer and looked up at her, keeping his expression neutral. She was still throttling the tea towel. "Oh? I'm afraid I don't understand, Maggie. What lies do you mean?"

"You know full well what I mean. You, YOU are the leaseholder of five acres of OUR land, and you told Thomas and me you weren't. Kindly explain yourself, Mr. Jenkins."

Burt noticed she didn't correct him on the use of her Christian name. "Ah, yes, I see." Burt was a little miffed and thought that they could have at least offered him a biscuit to go with the tea. "Maggie, my cows are healthy. They are above weight and show no sign of neglect. When you asked me if I knew the owner of the neglected and unhealthy cows that grazed on your property, I knew you couldn't be referring to me. I answered honestly."

She snorted in derision.

"However, if you'd asked me if I leased five acres of land on your property, then I would have told you that I did."

Tom opened his mouth to speak, but a quick look from his wife silenced him. He turned to Burt and shrugged.

"I think it best if we terminate the lease, Mr. Jenkins." She showed her teeth again, which confirmed to Burt she was indeed smiling. "Effective immediately."

"Do you mind if I pour another cup? I do enjoy Gunpowder Green," Burt asked politely.

She turned away and growled in frustration.

Mr. Warner leaned over and refilled both cups.

Burt raised his cup and took another sip. He saw the tea-towel tightly twisted and knotted in Maggie's pudgy hands and felt a pang of compassion for Tom. Again, he looked up at her. She hadn't moved, but her knuckles were stark white as she gripped the towel. "Alrighty, it's your land, but I'm paid up. By my calculations, for another nine months."

"How convenient, Mr. Jenkins," she snarled. "I've seen no records of that."

"I always paid old man Tim a year in advance. Have done so for ten years or thereabouts."

"The man was an irresponsible drunkard, which eventually killed him. He probably kept no records and, as I expect, neither do you."

Burt held her gaze and stood. He grabbed his hat from the seat beside him, took a deep breath, and slowly exhaled. "Old man Tim was a decent bloke, Maggie. He had his faults like most people do. He wasn't a saint, but a drunk he wasn't. Before you go spreading gossip get your facts right. Tim suffered from an ailing heart and that's what got him. He hadn't touched a drop of liquor in years. You see, he had an allergy to alcohol. The doctor called it an intolerance, or something like that. Drinking liquor gave him the runs and a rash, so Tim drank tea. His favourite blend was Gunpowder Green, he was the one who put me onto it."

Maggie's face turned scarlet. Burt thought the colour suited her, made her more human. "I'll be back in a few weeks with a receipt, and I appreciate the cuppa," Burt said. "I can find the door, thanks."

Burt tightened the cinch on the saddle and untethered his horse. Once mounted, he turned and rode down the path, happy to be going home.

A call made him turn. He looked over his shoulder and saw Tom waving goodbye.

Epilogue

It came as a bit of a surprise to Burt when he found his billy goat lying motionless on a rock beneath a sheltered overhang. He wasn't sure if he should be pleased or saddened. One thing was obvious, it died of natural causes and luckily the carcass had not begun to decompose yet. It was easier to take it home than to skin and bury it here in the rocky ground. With some difficulty, he loaded the billy onto the wagon and brought it back to his shed.

The carcass now hung from a hook. He'd expertly skinned it and draped the hide over a fence on the other side of his cottage, where he would later clean, salt, and roll it. He was now focused on butchering the meat for dog tucker and never heard Thomas Warner approach.

"Ya scared me half to death, Tom. I didn't hear you at all."

"Sorry, Mr. Jenkins, I thought you saw me."

Burt wiped his bloody hands on a rag. "Call me Burt, eh? And how have you been, Tom? Haven't seen you in a while, a month or so, I think."

Tom was silent a moment. "I, uh, I'm sorry for what happened. Maggie is …well, you know–"

"Nuff said. Don't worry about it, Tom," Burt interjected.

Tom was looking at the carcass swinging from the hook. "Maggie has been very upset lately…"

Burt looked up. "More than usual?"

"Intolerable."

"That's not good, eh?"

"The Angoras all finally gave birth."

"Congratulations. I'm sure Maggie is thrilled to bits."

"We have twelve kids running around creating mayhem."

"Kids are adorable, I'll give you that. It's when they're mature that it all changes," volunteered Burt.

"Yep, you're right, but the thing is, the offspring have black and brown fur and most have two white distinctive front feet that look like socks. They're not Angora white as they oughta be. Maggie was furious, she screamed for days and broke most of our crockery. She's still livid. Has made our lives bloody miserable. Seems as though a feral goat somehow got into the paddock and impregnated the nannies before we could stud it with an Angora billy."

Burt couldn't help himself and turned away from Tom, hoping to hide his grin. "That's a shame, Tom. Terrible," tut-tutted Burt, fighting to keep a straight face. He took a deep breath to steady himself.

Tom was silent and continued to stare at the carcass for a moment or two. "Looks like a goat."

"Yep, me billy finally croaked."

"If my memory serves me right, your billy had two white socks on its front feet, didn't it?"

Burt's eyes opened wide. Now it was his turn to remain silent as he focused on maintaining self-control. Feeling confident he could maintain his composure, he turned back to Tom, who looked very serious. Before he could say anything, Tom's face slowly cracked into a smile and, unable to hold back any longer, he burst out laughing. It was too much. Burt lost all restraint and joined in. Both men bent double, roaring in hilarity.

"Burt, you should have seen the look on her face when she first saw the newborn kids," cried Tom, gasping for air between fits of laughter. "… little white socks…" he slapped his hand on his thigh in hysterics.

This set Burt off even more and he laughed until he could hardly stand. With tears streaming down both their faces and their sides aching, both men staggered inside to have a cuppa.

148 Pastoral Road

Chapter One

Near Ohakune, 1963

The Empire Hotel wasn't a flash public hotel, even by moderate, rural New Zealand standards. The two-storied pub boasted four passably clean rooms for accommodation, a public bar, and, of course, for the ladies, a lounge with more civilized amenities. For convenience, the hotel's proprietor, Mr. Bernard Thompkins, also operated a bottle shop, on premises, to cater to those who preferred to do their drinking elsewhere. Out front, an assortment of dust-covered vehicles were parked. Most had seen better days and many leaked either oil, water, or both. The peacefulness of the small rural town was broken by an occasional outburst of barking as many utes had farm dogs tethered to them, but they were mostly ignored as their masters were otherwise occupied inside the establishment.

Mr. Thompkins, or Bernie to his patrons, was not a jolly fellow, nor gifted with a well-developed sense of humour. Few, if any, recalled ever seeing him smile, and most doubted they'd ever heard him laugh. Some suggested that two years earlier, when Willy rode his farm horse through the pub, was the last time that Bernie's face had cracked into a smile. After fathering five daughters, Willy's wife had finally given birth to a boy, and in celebration, he decided to let his mates know of the good news and clomped through the public bar on his horse shouting, "It's a boy!"

Someone claimed to have seen Bernie grin, but as far as stoic publicans went, Bernie kept the beer cold and flowing and that was what most people wanted.

As one would expect on a Friday afternoon, the public bar was full. The all-male occupants stood around chest-high tables, swilled beer, chatted loudly about this or that, and frequently offered opinions and ill-considered thoughts on various subjects, even if they knew nothing about them, which was quite often.

One tall, youngish man separated himself from his mates, close to where a pool table had once stood near the far wall, and clutching four empty jugs, headed for refills. Waiting for him behind the worn wooden bar was Sheryl.

Sheryl was by far the most attractive woman in town, and many an amorous bachelor, as well as one or two married men, had tried with less than encouraging results to ask her on a date and offered to take her to the pictures thirty miles away. All had failed miserably, and Sheryl made sure everyone knew that any romantic advances on her were unwelcome and fell on deaf ears.

However, the young man with the empty jugs was having quite a conversation with her, and she seemed in no hurry to replenish his beer as she chatted amicably. It didn't go unnoticed. His thirsty mates at the table watched with some surprise and elbowed each other with obvious amusement. Only when Bernie emerged from the Bottle Shop and gave her a testy look did Sheryl finally return to the business at hand.

"What the hell was all that about? Did ya ask her to marry you?"

teased Big Mike, a shearer originally from Taihape, when his friend finally returned, sloshing beer over the floor.

"You gotta get yourself a good woman, Rail," wisely offered Wiremu, a stock truck driver. "You're the only fulla not married, you can't stay single all your life."

There were grunts of agreement.

Thin and standing well over six foot four, Rail, a fencer on contract at a local sheep station, carefully poured beer into his glass and avoided eye contact with his friends. They were constantly badgering him to find a girlfriend, but there wasn't anyone nearby who interested him, and he wished they'd talk about something else.

"She's your bloody neighbour, mate, what more do you need? A written invitation?" goaded Willy. He drained his glass and wiped his mouth with the back of his hand.

"But you do like Sheryl, don't ya?" asked Big Mike.

Rail shrugged self-consciously. "Yeah, she's alright, I suppose."

"Why haven't you paid her a visit? She lives next bloody door to you," asked Big Mike.

It was common knowledge that Sheryl lived at 148 Pastoral Road, in a house belonging to the same farmer who owned the cottage next door that Rail occupied. When the shearing gangs came to town, the girls stayed with Sheryl, a cozy arrangement that suited both her and the farmer.

"I dunno. She works a lot in the evenings, so I don't see her at home often," said Rail dismissively. "Anyway, I don't think she wants to date blokes."

Rail's friends shared a look.

Big Mike leaned forward across the table and looked over his shoulder to ensure no one could overhear. "Ya know, Sheryl does like men."

Willy and Wiremu also took a step closer and nodded in agreement as Rail listened.

"She had a boyfriend a few years back, a logger. He died when a tree he was cutting fell on him, poor fella."

Rail winced.

"He lived in the same cottage you're renting."

"You're having me on."

"Is true," insisted Wiremu, nodding vigorously.

"It was quite a story," Big Mike went on. "They knew each other from here at the Empire. Anyway, at night, when she was home, she always drew the curtains closed. Then one night, she opens the curtains. The logger, I think his name was Lance, sees her inside her house and she in turn sees him and then waves for him to come over and pay her a visit." Big Mike paused as he refilled his glass.

"This a joke, isn't it?" Rail asked.

"Nope, is true," Big Mike stated emphatically.

Again, Wiremu and Willy's heads bobbed up and down in support.

Big Mike drained his glass and continued. "Next thing they've got a full-blown romance happening. Every time she wanted company, she'd open the curtains and that was their signal and the randy logger would pop over and see her."

"Until the tree fell on him," reminded Wiremu.

"Yep, that's the last time she was seen with a bloke. She took it badly," said Big Mike.

"That's sad for her," replied Rail.

"And for Lance," commiserated Wiremu.

"Ya wanna keep that in mind. The way she was flirting with you at the bar, I reckon you'll find them curtains open," added Big Mike with a grin. "Keep your eyes peeled." He gave Rail a nudge with his elbow and an encouraging wink.

The conversation turned to matters of national importance and rugby. Everyone was an expert and offered conflicting opinions on player selection and coaches, and before long they were arguing loudly as friends are apt to do.

Ignoring the raised voices, Rail looked towards the bar at Sheryl, who was serving a customer. He wouldn't admit it to anyone, but he did like her; she was fun to talk to and the few times he'd had a chat with her, it appeared they did have things in common and she didn't make him feel self-conscious or foolish. But then again, *what would she see in me?* He wondered.

With a sigh, Rail turned back to his mates. "You lot don't know what you're talking about."

Chapter Two

Rail was building a new fence line in the back-blocks on steep, recently cleared hills and by the time it was Friday, he was only too happy to visit his mates at the Empire. During the week, after arriving home from work, he would guiltily look out of his living room window and take a quick look over at Sheryl's. When she was home, he could see the lights on, but the curtains were always drawn. Some nights he caught himself looking more than once and wistfully imagined seeing her opening the curtains and seductively beckoning him to come over.

He missed female company. He enjoyed talking about this or that, and being alone offered no incentive to take care of himself. His mates were right; of his friends, he was the only one not married and even his parents pestered him about it. He could still hear his dad preaching to him when he last went to visit them. He'd be in his favourite chair with a couple of flagons in a case at his side. "You need a good woman, son, she'll make an honest man outa ya."

With some seriousness, his mum would look up from her ironing, nod in agreement, and always contribute: "Listen to your father, he knows what he's talking about."

He'd had a few girlfriends. The last one, Cindy was a bit too wild for his taste. She was a wool classer and after a long day and more than a few beers, began dancing on the board, slipped, and fell heavily onto the woolshed floor, breaking her arm. One of the shearers gave her another beer and a spare, then propped her up on the backseat of his Vauxhall and drove her to the doctor. She passed out before arriving. Not from the pain, but because she was plastered. She was still with the shearing gang, but moved to somewhere in Canterbury. He hadn't seen her in a year or so.

The feelings of loneliness always haunted him this time of the year. He felt old, and a loving relationship with a woman he cared for seemed more remote with every passing season, but he'd get over it as he always did.

Of course, there were other women in town. Most were married, and those who were single had boyfriends. The pickings were slim. Betsy, who worked in the post office, had a nasty skin rash that looked like someone had dragged her face down along the road. He couldn't imagine cuddling up to her on the sofa and giving her a passionate kiss. The only other candidate was Maureen, a bad-tempered widow who worked part-time at the dairy. She spent more time in the Empire's lounge bar drinking shandys than she did at home. So that really just left Sheryl. He looked out of the window towards 148 Pastoral Road one last time before he left for the pub, but she wasn't there. "She's at work," he said aloud as he climbed into his Land Rover.

Rail always parked in the same spot. It was easily identifiable by a large oil stain, and as he screeched to a stop, he saw Sheryl's car, which confirmed she was at work. He smiled.

"Where have ya been? Did we do something to piss you off?" asked Big Mike as he emptied a jug of beer into his glass.

"I've been workin' up in the back-blocks, been too busy to come down here," Rail replied.

"Is tough goin' up in them hills," Willy replied. "Better you than me."

As if rehearsed, Rail's mates, in perfect synchronization, raised their arms in salute and downed their glasses.

"My shout," offered Rail as he scooped three empty jugs into his hands and walked to the bar.

Immediately, his friends began a whispered conversation while keeping half an eye on Rail, who was having a friendly chat with Sheryl. It didn't last long. Bernie was stacking newly washed jugs onto a rack. When Sheryl laughed, Bernie gave her a cough. A subtle reminder that empty glasses needed collecting and tables had to be wiped.

Disappointed at having his chat with Sheryl cut short, Rail returned with four full jugs and a glass for himself. His mates were unusually quiet.

It was Big Mike who spoke. "Isn't it your birthday soon?"

Rail looked up. "You speaking to me?"

"Yeah, who else?" Big Mike asked.

Willy and Wiremu watched and said nothing.

"Not for another couple of days. It's on Sunday. Why?"

"No reason. I just remembered you saying something about it a couple of weeks ago," Mike said.

"Well, did Sheryl open the curtains for you?" Wiremu asked with a laugh, changing the subject.

Rail shook his head.

"You have to keep an eye open, Rail, or you'll miss your chance. I reckon she fancies you, the way she's chatting you up. Just you wait and see, it will happen. I have a sixth sense about it," advised Wiremu.

"He does," Willy nodded in support. "He has EPS. Remember how he predicted the score on the last test match? And he said I'd have a boy, and he was right."

Big Mike smiled. "ESP, Willy, not EPS."

"Same thing. Anyway, I believe in that stuff."

Rail turned away and glanced towards the bar. Sheryl must have sensed him looking; she gave a smile and a little wave.

His mates laughed and Rail's heart beat a little faster.

Big Mike missed nothing and saw her reaction. "I told you, she fancies you, Rail," he laughed.

Rail felt his cheeks redden. Just then he felt a hand on his back. He turned and saw Betsy standing beside him.

"Rail, you have a parcel at the post office waiting for you," she told him.

"Oh, thanks, Betsy."

"You can pick it up tomorrow morning." She smiled and walked back towards the lounge.

"Right'o," he shouted after her, "thanks!"

"Nice gal, shame about that rash though. And a package…?" Big Mike wondered.

"Yeah, that will be from Mum. She always mails me socks and undies on my birthday," Rail said.

"My Mum always sends me a tie for my birthday," volunteered Willy. "Got a drawer full of them and never worn one. I use them for Christmas decorations and hang them on the tree. The kids love 'em, and they look good."

"I don't even own a tie," said Big Mike.

"Your shout," said Wiremu to Big Mike as he emptied the last jug.

Chapter Three

Saturday was fairly typical for Rail. He woke early, did his washing, mowed the lawn, and drove into town before the post office closed at lunchtime to pick up the package his mother mailed. As he accurately guessed, it was socks, undies, and a birthday card.

A few times throughout the day he caught himself looking over at Sheryl's. She was at home, but he didn't see her. He wondered if his mates were just pulling his leg about the curtains. It wouldn't surprise him. They were always clowning around and playing practical jokes on people.

Early afternoon was uneventful, and later he went to the local rugby field and watched a game, then spent a couple of hours having a few beers at the club rooms. He decided not to visit the Empire and returned home for a quiet night. He knew Sheryl was working as it was Saturday night, but he couldn't help himself and peeked anyway. As he expected, the lights were off and the curtains were closed.

He woke on Sunday morning feeling a little sad. It was his birthday and he was going to spend it alone. He had no invites from his mates, no girlfriend to come over, and no one to share his birthday with. He thought that maybe he'd take the dog and go pig hunting, but some nasty clouds approaching from the south changed his mind. He didn't want to get caught out in the bush when the weather turned ugly. Instead, he changed the oil in his Land Rover. It was long overdue, and he'd been meaning to get to it for weeks but kept putting it off.

Sunday was spent in solitude and quiet reflection. He did a few odd jobs around the house and cleaned a little, then sat outside in the sun with a cold beer and read the paper.

After dinner he decided to clean his rifle. He hadn't given it a thorough going-over since it was last used, and it needed a good wipe-down badly. He rose from his armchair to retrieve the gun and, as he walked past the window, casually looked out. He stopped, walked back, and looked again. Sure enough, the lights were on and the curtains were open! Rail froze as a million thoughts invaded his mind. He stared open-mouthed. *What the heck*?

He recalled the conversations at the pub and what his mates had told him - he shook his head in disbelief. The open curtains meant nothing, surely it was just a coincidence. His mates were pulling his leg; the whole curtain thing was nothing more than a lark, a joke being played on him. Reluctantly, he turned away, retrieved his rifle, oil, and rags, and returned to his chair.

The gun lay on his lap, still fully assembled, however, his thoughts were on Sheryl. He couldn't help himself. Again, he rose from his seat and walked to the window for another look. The curtains were still open. *Were the open curtains a signal, a genuine invitation to come over*? he wondered. He stood staring in confusion and indecision when she appeared, backlit and framed in the window. She didn't move for a moment, and then raised her arm and waved, and his heart began to race. He felt his face redden and didn't know how to respond. He raised his arm and weakly waved back, but more in politeness than anything else. He felt foolish standing at the window and was about to return to his chair when she beckoned him with her hand. It was an unmistakable and very clear invite. Blood rushed to his head and he felt his legs tremble. "OK," he said weakly, forgetting she couldn't hear him. She beckoned again and this time, without thought or a conscious decision, his arm rose and waved in acknowledgment. *Shit, what have I done?*

"I'll need a bloody bath," he said to himself, leaving the rifle on the chair. "Can't go over there smelling like a rubbish tip… dirty bugger."

He ran the water, stripped off, and before long was soaking in the tub and thinking about the unexpected invitation. Again, he felt his heart begin to race as he vigorously scrubbed his skin raw.

Feeling remarkably clean, he toweled off and saw the birthday package from his mum. He grinned as he stepped into brand-new socks and undies. For the first time in months he felt excited, happy, and found himself smiling as he prepared to visit Sheryl. If his mates at the Empire only knew… he laughed and couldn't wait to tell them. Although they probably wouldn't believe him anyway.

After brushing his teeth, he took a moment to reflect in case he forgot something, and then remembered. Cindy had once given him a fancy bottle of Old Spice. It sat in a drawer and has never been used, and he wondered if it was still good. Did aftershave go off after a while? He unscrewed the cap and took a whiff, then coughed. It seemed to be OK. He poured a sizeable amount on his hand, and then a bit more, just to be sure, and slapped it on. He now had a measure of sympathy for sheep and understood how they felt when dipped.

He slipped on his freshly laundered and best swanni, then ran a comb through his hair and stared into the mirror. He felt his heart pounding. He was nervous and wanted to create a good impression. For some reason, it mattered and was important that she knew he'd made the effort to be presentable for her.

Once outside, he climbed into his Red Bands and as he walked down the driveway, he realized he should bring something, a little gift, a token of his appreciation – but nothing extravagant. He didn't want to overdo it. He stopped and gave the matter some thought. By the light of the moon, he saw the overgrown and neglected hydrangea plant that sat at the end of the driveway. Many of its large flowers had seen better days, but there were still a few good ones remaining. With a pocketknife he cut three stems, and with the huge bluish-coloured flowers firmly grasped in his hand he trudged up the path to Sheryl's place.

The front of the house was in darkness, and the only light came from rooms around the back. His heart beat furiously and he was surprised she did not hear it thumping. He swallowed and wiped his clammy free hand on his pants before climbing the two steps onto the porch and knocking firmly.

The door opened with a creak and, lit by the moon, she stood framed in the doorway. She wore a dress; he'd never seen her in anything but jeans before. Her hair was loose and styled nicely. *My gosh, she is beautiful*, he thought.

"G'day Rail," she said with a smile, "c'mon in."

He kicked off his boots and before he could say a word, she moved aside and turned on the light.

"SURPRISE!"

Rail froze.

"HAPPY BIRTHDAY!"

What the…? His head swiveled in every direction as he took in the sight before him.

Her living room was filled with people, his friends. There was Big Mike sucking on a beer and grinning. Wiremu and his lovely wife, Tania. Even Willy and Sue were here; they must have found a babysitter. He saw Betsy from the post office, Maureen from the dairy, and even Bernie from the pub, who held a saucer of asparagus rolls. He may have smiled, or it could have been a grimace, it was hard to tell. There were a few others from the rugby club… all his friends. Sheryl's house was full. The kitchen table had been moved into the corner and was adorned with lamingtons, sausage rolls, asparagus rolls, and a birthday cake someone had made.

Rail felt his face redden and stood awkwardly with his hydrangeas clasped tightly behind his back. He was stunned and didn't know what to do. He turned to Sheryl, who was beaming. Someone put a record on, and next thing he heard the song *Walk like a Man* thunder from the speakers.

He felt foolish.

Sheryl saw the flowers he was attempting to hide. "Are they for me?" she asked, saving him from further embarrassment.

With blushing cheeks, he awkwardly handed them over.

"You're so sweet! Thank you, Rail." She leaned forward and kissed him. Just a peck on the cheek, but it was a kiss nonetheless. Big Mike saw it and, with a whoop, began dancing with Betsy.

Someone thrust a bottle of beer into Rail's hand, and he stood self-consciously near the door as everyone wished him a happy birthday and slapped him on the back.

"Geezus, Rail, you bloody reek," bellowed Big Mike. "Were you dipping sheep this afo?"

Sheryl saw his discomfort. "Is Old Spice, and I love it," she quickly answered.

Before he could respond, she grabbed his hand and pulled him after her, weaving through the dancers and leading him into the kitchen. She closed the door, faced him, and placed both hands on his chest. "Rail," she began, "I'm sorry, it was their idea, not mine. They put me up to it and… I knew it would cause you embarrassment. I didn't want that to happen. I like and respect you too much to see you hurt." She opened her mouth to say more, then changed her mind and turned away to open a cupboard. She reached in, pulled out a vase, and began filling it with water. "They're beautiful, thank you, Rail."

Rail was disappointed and felt deflated, but he knew he needed to get over it. He slowly let out his breath and forced himself to relax as he watched her. Yes, he'd been tricked, and it was a cruel joke, but he should've known better than letting himself be sucked in. His friends meant him no harm, and neither did Sheryl. All they wanted to do was surprise him with a birthday party. He continued to look at her as she placed the flowers in the vase… *so beautiful*, he thought wistfully.

As if hearing him, she looked up and smiled.

"The Old Spice is a bit much, isn't it?" he said with a laugh.

Epilogue

Monday was a bit of a slog for Rail. He woke with a headache and a queasy stomach and it wasn't until lunchtime that he began to feel human again. He'd been carrying fence posts up steep hill country and believed the strenuous exercise helped him overcome his hangover. However, his thoughts were on Sheryl and the party the evening before.

He'd arrived home around midnight, well past his Sunday night bedtime, after a lovely time with his friends. They'd gone to considerable lengths to surprise him on his birthday and succeeded, although causing him some embarrassment and making him lose his dignity. He was still a little peeved at being tricked by Sheryl and knew his mates would needle him about it for weeks, but she had been a real angel and made him feel welcome. He'd spent most of the night dancing with her and thoroughly enjoyed himself.

He sat on a huge rock covered with moss and lichen. From his position, he had a bird's eye view of a large valley and watched sheep grazing far below. Not far away a hawk lazily circled. He watched it for a short while, but it didn't come near, and with a single lethargic wing flap, glided off in another direction. His thoughts returned to Sheryl and he wondered if she enjoyed herself last night… or, more to the point, whether she enjoyed his company. She hadn't said anything, nor had she given any clue to her feelings about him. He threw a rock down the hill and watched it bounce again and again until it splashed into the creek at the bottom. Perhaps he needed to grow up, stop acting like a lovesick schoolboy, and forget about her. He wearily rose from the rock and looked up to where he needed to build the fence-line.

By the time he arrived home, it was just getting dark. It had been a long day and he was tired. He was cleaning the kitchen after dinner when he looked out of the window and saw that Sheryl's curtains were open. It took him by surprise, and he paused for a moment.

"Nope. Once bitten, twice shy," he said quietly to himself and sat down to read the newspaper.

He couldn't focus on reading, however, and risked another quick peek. To his astonishment, she stood silhouetted in the window and waved at him, then gestured – an obvious invitation. He turned away and began pacing, and instantly felt his cheeks flush as the memory of last evening's humiliation resurfaced. He didn't know what to think; his mind was in absolute turmoil. He tried to reason with himself.

It wasn't her fault. She apologized profusely as she explained how Big Mike had put her up to it. 'It was the only way to get you out of the house,' he recalled her saying. He looked again. She hadn't moved, and waved again when she saw him reappear.

"Alright, so be it," he said with finality and walked to the door. He stepped outside, slid into his Red Bands, and clumped to the hedge bordering her house. He looked over the top to see the area in front of the woolshed where everyone hid their cars last night, but the space was empty, not a vehicle in sight. She was alone.

He leaned against a fencepost and rubbed the stubble on his chin. He wouldn't bathe or change his clothes; he'd go over and see her just the way he was after a hard day of work. If they were playing another joke on him, he'd let them have it. He wasn't going to be suckered in a second time.

With his heart racing, he trudged past his Land Rover and down the driveway, ignoring the overgrown hydrangea, and turned into her place. As he approached, the door opened. This time a light was on in the living room and she stood looking at him. With eyes glistening, she silently watched as he climbed onto the porch, and as he was about to speak, she stepped forward and threw her arms around him.

A Flaming Mess

Chapter One

Far North, 1963

The local dairy stood at the corner of Crooks Road and Pohutukawa Drive in a small community, inhabited by less than two hundred people, in the North Island's remote far north. Accessible only through a winding, unsealed gravel road and prone to frequent closures during winter, either by slips or washouts, the village was mostly forgotten about or just plainly overlooked.

A dozen or so wild horses roamed freely and grazed without impediment along the grass roadside verges of the sleepy district. Neighborhood dogs had long since given up barking at the horses, and for most of the animals, like the residents, they were left alone to their own devices and did pretty much as they pleased.

A beautiful coastline offered access to exceptional fishing and a variety of small boats and runabouts lay tethered to buoys, bobbing peacefully in the calm waters of the sheltered bay. Fishing provided a modest income to those who felt the need to work, or as a leisure activity to just pass the time.

The dairy was the daily focal point for the residents. Mr. Prakash owned and operated the dairy in a friendly and efficient manner, along with his wife, mother-in-law, and five children. Mr. Prakash and his family had arrived from Fiji some years previously on a work visa and decided to stay in New Zealand after his contract ended. They purchased the dairy, along with the attached house, about seven years ago, and Mr. and Mrs. Prakash worked hard to provide for his children and to keep their family and community safe.

He opened the dairy at 7:00 a.m. seven days a week and locked the door promptly at 9:00 p.m. each night. Mrs. Prakash believed that in addition to closing on Christmas day, the only day they were shut, the shop should also close on the Queen's birthday. Mr. Prakash disagreed, believing the loss of income would be too great and suggested his wife's sentiments arose only because of the recent and much publicized visit to New Zealand by Her Majesty, Queen Elizabeth II. Mrs. Prakash tactfully decided to drop the request, rather than risk a squabble.

On entering the dairy, the counter was strategically situated along the right-hand wall so that Mr. Prakash could observe his customers. Additionally, he had positioned mirrors so he could keep a close eye on shoppers that he couldn't see directly from the counter. Not trusting his eagle eyes alone for security, he also placed on a shelf behind the stool where he sat, beside the decorative tins of Aulsbrooks, Iced Animal Biscuits, half-a-dozen small Hindu deities, figurines that offered spiritual protection. Shoplifting, as it turned out, was infrequent but not totally unheard of.

45

Perched on his stool, atop his tasseled pillow, Mr. Prakash could observe comings and goings with ease and aid any customer requiring his help.

This particular morning was no different from any other until two newcomers arrived. Their unexpected entry into his dairy prompted one of Mr. Prakash's eyebrows to rise in silent question. He didn't normally have many strangers here. He greeted the young couple cordially with a friendly head nod and continued to read the *Fiji Times* newspaper sent to him monthly by his sister. Every fifteen seconds or so, he'd raise his head and establish where the customers were and what they were up to. Judging from their loud exclamations and laughter, he determined they were Australians.

They were holding up a jar of Marmite and daring each other to purchase the sandwich spread and eat it for lunch. *Kids,* he thought with a slight shake of his head. More customers entered, and in no time the dairy was full.

Both Australians approached the counter. "Do you sell Golden Gaytime ice-cream? It's on a stick."

"No, no," replied Mr. Prakash quickly as he put aside his newspaper. "You buy Jelly Tip, is good," he suggested, offering a tempting alternative as he didn't wish to miss out on a sale.

The Aussies looked puzzled.

Mr. Prakash pried himself from his stool and walked from behind the counter to the freezer near the back wall. He lifted the lid and extracted two Jelly Tip ice-cream bars. "Very, very, good," he beamed.

"Alrighty, then, we'll give it a go," said the male Aussie after receiving an encouraging nod from his female companion.

Mr. Prakash squeezed past other customers, returned to his stool, and took the money from the outstretched hand of the Australian. He counted out the change and turned to Mrs. Tuhana, who'd been waiting patiently. He saw the back of two other customers, quickly departing without having purchased anything. His brows furrowed in suspicion.

"Busy this morning," Mrs. Tuhana said, watching the tourists leave. She left the dairy carrying two loaves of bread.

"Have a good day!" he called after her.

Mr. Prakash twisted on his seat to record the sale into an exercise book. It was where he accounted for each local's tab – what they owed him. Once a month they would settle in full. However, the book wasn't there.

Another customer approached the counter. "Good morning, Mr. Prakash."

"Uh, good morning, Bill. How's the fishing today?" He looked on the floor but

couldn't see the bright red cover of the book. *Perhaps I kicked it under the counter*, he thought.

"Just this, that'll do, eh?" Bill held up a tin of baked beans and another of spaghetti. "No luck today, maybe tomorrow it will improve."

"Uh, yes, tomorrow, eh?" Mr. Prakash was flustered. He found his pencil and hastily wrote Bill's purchase on a paper bag, and then noted Mrs. Tuhana's purchase of two loaves of bread. The shop was finally empty, and he was perplexed.

He called his wife, and together they looked everywhere for the red exercise book with the neatly laid out columns of numbers alongside local customers' names. It had vanished.

"Did someone steal it?" Mrs. Prakash asked, finally suggesting what neither of them wanted to acknowledge. Along with his mother-in-law, Mr. Prakash and his wife searched again, but the book was nowhere to be found.

Once more behind the counter, Mr. Prakash automatically scanned the shelves, looking for anything untoward. His head slowly turned from item to item and stopped at the chicken chips. He always made sure that four bags of each type of potato chips were on the shelf. However, two bags were missing, and he knew he hadn't sold any since he restocked the shelf the previous evening. His immediate thoughts turned to the young Australian couple. Could they have taken his book and the chips? He quickly dismissed the notion.

An hour later, Reggie Palmer arrived at the dairy, running and out of breath. Mr. Prakash looked up from his newspaper in surprise as the elderly man stormed in.

"Did you see anyone suspicious hanging around?" asked Mr. Palmer. His cheeks were red from the exertion.

"Oh dear, what happened? Is something wrong?" Mr. Prakash asked.

"Some bloody mongrel broke into my ute, took the radio."

Mr. Prakash looked sympathetic. "Only strangers here were Aussies, two of them, about an hour ago. When did this happen?"

"This mornin' sometime. Not sure of the time, cause we were out fishing and only now returned and saw the damage. The bastards broke the window and ripped out the radio."

Mr. Prakash thought about his accounting book and the two

packets of missing chicken-flavoured chips and wondered if the events were related. He wasn't sure and chose not to say anything.

He shook his head. "Only the Aussies."

"What do they look like?"

Chapter Two

The police car safely navigated the winding road, dodged a swayback, piebald mare that stood in the middle of the street, and turned slowly onto Crooks Road. Mr. Prakash watched the car disappear around the corner and assumed Mr. Palmer had called the police about his stolen car radio. He knew the police would eventually turn up at the dairy; everyone did.

As he predicted, half an hour later a young, pimple-faced constable stepped into the dairy, paused a moment, and then turned towards the counter. "Good morning. Are you the owner?"

"How can I help you?" replied Mr. Prakash with a practiced smile.

"I'm investigating a burglary and hoped you could answer a few questions for me."

"Of course, happy to assist with you."

"Have you seen anyone suspicious hanging around?"

"Oh, uh, not really," Mr. Prakash said. He scratched his chin. "Two strangers were here this morning, a young couple, Australian tourists, I think. But they were not suspicious."

The constable flicked a notebook open. "Can you describe their appearance?"

"Uh, a young man and a woman, in their early twenties–"

"Tell them about the book and chips!" exclaimed Mrs. Prakash.

She'd been listening near the doorway to their home at the rear of the dairy.

"Ahh, is nothing," her husband replied, waving a hand dismissively in her direction.

The constable turned from one to the other and finally, his eyes settled on Mr. Prakash. "Book? Chips?"

"I have lost a book I use to record customer purchases, and two packets of chicken chips are missing."

"They were stolen," Mrs. Prakash added, walking to the counter. "Someone took the book, yes?" She folded her arms.

"This book, you record what the customer buys and–"

"–And then they pay me monthly," Mr. Prakash said.

"Let me ask you something. What is the total amount of money you are owed that is recorded in the book?"

"Eighty-three pounds, four shillings, and sixpence," replied Mr. Prakash without pause.

The constable whistled and scratched away quickly in his notebook. "That's a lot of money."

Mr. Prakash shrugged and scowled at his wife for mentioning the missing book.

"Uh, these tourists, what clothes were they wearing?"

"The woman wore jeans and a tee-shirt, and he, uh, shorts and a tee-shirt. But I don't think they–"

"Thank you, Mr...." The constable inclined his head.

"Prakash, Mr. Prakash."

"Thank you, Mr. Prakash. I believe the burglary and your stolen book might be–"

"And chicken chips," added Mrs. Prakash.

"Yes, and chicken chips… may be related. We will investigate the matter. May I have your contact details, please?"

Two children walked into the dairy and up to the counter. After looking curiously at the policeman, they stared hungrily through the display cabinet at the assortment of lollies. Mrs. Prakash gave the constable all the details he needed while the children um'd and ah'd over their choices. Mr. Prakash filled a small paper bag with a delectable assortment and took a sixpence from them.

Outside a few more people gathered and wondered what was going on. It wasn't every day a policeman arrived here. Some suspected it had to do with Reggie Palmer's stolen radio. Patsy Klinger stood knowingly, with arms folded, and informed everyone that Moonies were looking to settle in the community and would force people either to join their cult or to move elsewhere.

Around the corner on Pohutukawa Drive, about a mile from the dairy, a dilapidated house, surrounded by old broken-down cars, a bus with its rear wheels missing, and an old, rusted truck faced the bay. Inside, the three Burgess brothers were enjoying the last of their beer. The oldest brother, Bruce, had recently returned home after being released from Mount Crawford Prison in Wellington. He'd been convicted of burglary and aggravated assault and sentenced to thirty months' detention.

On his release, Bruce returned to his family home in the far north and moved in with his brothers. Both parents had died in a tragic boating accident five years previously, when their small runabout crashed into the rocks at the entrance to the bay. The coroner had deemed excessive alcohol had contributed to the outcome. Interestingly, no one was overly saddened or disagreed with the coroner, as the Burgess family were well-known boozers that had plagued the community for years.

The brothers hadn't worked for some time and relied heavily on the unemployment benefit to purchase necessities like beer and drugs. While all three brothers were capable of working, neither was willing. Previous employers described them as lazy and dishonest.

Since celebrating the release and arrival of older brother Bruce, they had quickly spent the last of their money on beer and the realization that they had no more until the following week only just dawned on them. Bruce stood at the window looking out across the bay, while the other two brothers, Hamish and Sean, sat on the stained sofa and looked morose. Two empty bags of chicken-flavoured potato chips lay beside them amongst other discarded food wrappers and rubbish,

"I don't know what you're whining about. Look how much money I saved you by nicking the book from the dairy," Bruce laughed and thrust out his chest. "Everyone here owes us a debt of thanks as no one needs to pay their bloody bill."

"That's all very well, but what do we do now? All our money is gone," chimed in Hamish. He picked the book up and quickly flicked through the pages.

"We'll drive to Kaitaia a little later and flog off the radio. I know a guy there, he'll buy it." Bruce watched a young couple climb from a van and begin to walk around the headland at the end of the road. "Who are these guys? When did they move here?"

Hamish dropped the book, pried himself from the sofa, and walked to the window. "Dunno. Haven't seen them before. Must be tourists or something."

Sean made his way over to the window and stood beside his brothers. "They were in the dairy earlier. Sounded like Aussies to me."

"Is that right? Fair dinkum," Bruce laughed again, then up-ended the bottle of beer before wiping his mouth and belching. "There goes another." He tossed the bottle onto the sofa where it bounced off and fell onto the floor. No one seemed to care. He saw the book from the dairy. "Best if we burn that book."

"Why? Is interesting to read how much money people owe the dairy," Hamish said.

"Cause it's evidence," replied Bruce. "Chuck the bloody thing in the fireplace and burn it." He turned back to the window and looked up the road at the van belonging to the Aussies. "C'mon, I have an idea."

Chapter Three

"Did anyone see in which direction the young tourist couple went?" asked the constable once he was outside the dairy.

Patsy Klinger pointed towards Pohutukawa Drive. "They went that way. I saw them driving a kombi van."

Others nodded in agreement. "Did they steal the radio?" someone asked.

At that moment a noisy car drove past. The driver and two other passengers stared at the constable with mouths agape.

Two kids, their mouths full of lollies, watched curiously.

"Bloody Moonies," stated Patsy once the loud car with a leaky exhaust had passed and she could be heard again.

"I just need to ask them a couple of questions. They can assist us with our inquiries," informed the constable as he removed his hat and climbed into his patrol car.

The radio didn't work, as he was too far away from base. Constable Ngata scratched his head. This call-out was proving to be a little more than a simple burglary. He turned his head as someone tapped on his window. He opened the door.

"There they are!" exclaimed the woman who'd been standing outside the dairy. "Those Moonies." She pointed behind him.

Sure enough, the two Australian tourists were running towards him. "Officer! Officer!"

He stepped from his car as the young couple approached.

"Someone broke into our van!"

"Whoa, hang on a tick. What happened?"

"We went for a walk around the bay and when we got back the side window was smashed and our stuff was scattered outside!" exclaimed the man as he bent over to catch his breath. "We saw three blokes running away."

"You witnessed three men breaking into your van?" asked Constable Ngata.

"Well, no, but they were running away. Had to be them, as we didn't see anyone else."

"Alright, climb in. Let's go and have a look, shall we?"

"Don't know why you're going that way," Patsy Klinger said. "The guys you want just drove off in that noisy car… is the Burgess boys, bloody no-hopers."

The two Australians climbed in the backseat of the patrol car as Constable Ngata turned to Patsy. "Burgess boys?"

"Yeah, they just drove past in that loud Morris Oxford," she said.

"They live here?"

"Yep, the place with the bus and old truck outside. Just around the corner," she informed him.

Constable Ngata had no desire to drive after three men by himself when he had no proof they had committed any crime. No one had actually witnessed them breaking into the van, therefore they were only suspects, but he wanted to talk to them nonetheless. As he knew where they lived, they'd undoubtedly return, and he could come back here and bring help. Meanwhile, he needed to clear up the radio burglary and the theft from the dairy.

"Thank you," he said.

As described, the possessions of the Australians were strewn on the grass outside the Volkswagen van. As far as they could tell, nothing had been stolen, as the tourists kept their travel cheques and cash on them.

Constable Ngata questioned them in detail and confirmed they had been in the dairy. It seemed unlikely they had stolen the accounting book. However, they believed that two of the three men who later ran away from their van were inside the dairy during the time they were there.

"Describe the clothing they wore," asked the constable.

"One wore blue overalls, the other a red chequered shirt and jeans."

Constable Ngata diligently wrote the details in his notepad and then searched through the van and items scattered on the ground, but didn't see a radio or an accounting book. Satisfied that the two Australians hadn't committed a crime, he took their details, asked them about their travel plans, and allowed them to be on their way.

He cruised slowly along Pohutukawa Drive towards the Burgess house. It was easy to identify with the old bus and truck standing next to it. He parked out front, slowly walked through long grass and garbage towards the door, and knocked. As he expected, no one replied.

He walked around the back, weaving around junk and unidentifiable rusted hulks, and saw no indication anyone was home. He made his way to the front of the house again and peered through the living room window. What a mess.

Beer bottles and rubbish littered the floor. On the sofa, he saw two empty bags of chicken chips. It all began to make sense. He returned to his car and drove back to the dairy.

Constable Ngata waited until Mr. Prakash finished serving a customer.

"Good day, Mrs. Wirihana," said Mr. Prakash as he finished recording the sale.

She gave the constable a nod and exited the dairy to stop and chat with Patsy Klinger, who was still outside.

"How can I help, constable?" asked Mr. Prakash.

Mrs. Prakash and her mother stepped into the shop from the doorway at the rear of the dairy to listen.

"Earlier, when you were serving the young Australian couple, you told me there were others in the shop."

"Oh yes. There were more people," nodded Mr. Prakash.

"Can you describe what the two people you didn't recognize were wearing? The ones who were in the shop but didn't buy anything."

"Oh dear, uh, let me think on this. I didn't see their faces, but both were men." Mr. Prakash scratched his thinning scalp. "I am thinking that one had a red shirt. The other… uh, perhaps a blue shirt, I am not sure … but yes, blue."

"Could they have been overalls?"

"Ah yes, indeed," he nodded and smiled. "Overalls."

"Are you familiar with the Burgess family?" asked Constable Ngata.

Mr. Prakash's face clouded over. He nodded again. "Hamish and Sean, yes, but the other one, I don't really know him, as he hasn't been around here much. Not nice people."

"It was them, wasn't it?" asked Mrs. Prakash. She stepped closer.

Mr. Prakash's mouth tightened.

"We can't jump to any conclusions. We need to talk to them first. How much do they owe you, Mr. Prakash?"

"Oh, dear. Twelve pounds, two shillings," he replied quickly.

"You memorize all the accounting?" smiled the constable, impressed at the memory of Mr. Prakash.

"He knows everything when it comes to money," answered Mrs. Prakash.

Constable Ngata turned as Reggie Palmer entered the dairy.

"Did ya get them thieve'n Aussie bastards?" he asked.

"Wasn't them, Mr. Palmer," replied the constable.

"Oh. Who then?"

"Hamish and Sean," offered Mr. Prakash.

"And the oldest one, Bruce, most likely. He just got out of prison," suggested Reggie, who was scowling. "I shoulda bloody known." He made brief eye contact with Mr. Prakash.

"Bruce Burgess was just released from prison?" queried the constable.

"Yep, sure was. He came back here a couple of nights ago."

Constable Ngata wrote the new information in his pad. "We don't know for sure it's them. So be careful who you accuse," he warned.

"It'll be them alright," affirmed Reggie.

"I'll be back tomorrow. Please, keep our chat to ourselves, eh? No need to go alarming anyone. What do you say, Mr. Prakash? Mr. Palmer?"

"I won't say anything," Reggie agreed.

Mr. Prakash nodded.

Chapter Four

Two patrol cars holding three constables and a senior constable drove quickly towards the small village. Trailing behind, a parole officer did his best to keep up, but the dust was thick and reduced visibility. Their progress was slowed by half a dozen horses that stood in the middle of the road near the dairy. Honking the horn did little to faze the animals, who merely raised their heads, looked insolently at the police cars, and refused to move. Finally, one car nudged forward and the horse reluctantly moved aside, allowing the small convoy to drive on.

The urgency was compounded by a thick column of smoke that rose, caught the onshore breeze, and then dissipated inland. Constable Ngata drove quickly around the corner onto Pohutukawa Drive and immediately saw the source of the smoke.

"Bloody hell!" exclaimed Senior Constable Talbot, who rode with Constable Ngata. Nearly all the residents of the community stood at a safe distance from the burning house and watched the fierce blaze destroy the Burgess home. It appeared to have been burning for some time, as there wasn't much of the house left standing. Even as they parked, a wall collapsed in a shower of sparks and the locals cheered. There were no other buildings nearby and nothing else was in danger of catching fire.

"What the dickens is going on here?" questioned Constable Ngata, speaking to no one in particular as he and the senior constable stepped from their car. He saw Reggie Palmer and walked towards him. "Mr. Palmer, what happened? Is there anyone inside? Why isn't the fire brigade here?"

"Morning, Constable," greeted Reggie cheerfully. He nodded at the senior constable. "Yeah, well, about 7:00 a.m. this morning the house, uh, just caught fire. No one is inside, the Burgess boys didn't return last night. Who woulda thought... Bit of a coincidence, eh?"

"Just – caught – fire? Where is the fire department?" asked Senior Constable Talbot.

"Oh, well, you see, officer, what's the point? It will take them about forty-five minutes to get here and by then it'll be too late. Might as well let the fire burn what it can. Does us all a favour, doesn't it?" he grinned.

"What do you mean?" asked Senior Constable Talbot.

"No point in the Burgess boys coming back here when there's nothing to come back to, and we're spared from having the no-hopers around here creating misery and causing trouble."

Others began gathering around and protesting the behaviour of the Burgess brothers.

"Any idea as to the cause of the fire?" asked the senior constable. He looked from face to face and was met with smiles. The atmosphere was almost festive.

Most people shook their heads.

"Bit of a mystery, that," replied Reggie. "All those junky cars and flammable liquid, coulda been anything... bad wiring."

"We are required to investigate. Arson is a serious offense," said the senior constable, trying to look stern.

"And so you should. Can't go having lawbreakers around here," Reggie agreed. A few bystanders echoed his sentiment.

"Could've been the Moonies. They're on drugs," volunteered Patsy Klinger.

The four constables gathered in a small group away from everyone. "Was arson, no question," exclaimed Senior Constable Talbot. "Not much we can do here. Let's go back to the station and contact the Fire Service." He turned to Constable Ngata. "You stay, hang around, someone might let something slip... you never know, and the Burgess brothers might yet return."

"Nothing here for me to do. I may as well leave," grizzled the parole officer, then climbed into his car and drove off.

The fire brigade eventually turned up about two hours later and hosed down smoldering embers, but for the most part, the fire had burned itself out. There wasn't much to see anymore and, bored with the spectacle, the locals had wandered off. The Burgess home had been completely destroyed; nothing remained except a few blackened timbers and rusty sheets of corrugated iron. Thankfully, no one had seen the Burgess brothers since they'd driven off the day before.

Epilogue

Mr. Prakash was stocking his shelves when Constable Ngata entered the dairy. He looked up and gave the constable a warm smile. "All is good, yes?" He kept his right hand at his side and out of sight.

"Hello, Mr. Prakash. I thought I would drop by and give you some news."

"Oh, is good news, I am hoping."

"Along with the fire department investigators, we searched through the remains of the Burgess house looking for the cause of the fire."

"Yes."

"An accelerant was used. It was arson."

Mr. Prakash looked puzzled.

"Petrol, someone used petrol to put the house on fire," the constable explained.

"Oh, dear me," tut-tutted Mr. Prakash.

"I don't think we will ever find out who did it."

Mr. Prakash nodded in agreement.

"On a happier note, the Burgess brothers were apprehended just south of Kaitaia while they tried to steal a car. They won't be a problem for you or anyone here anymore," said the constable.

"This is good."

"Oh yes, I almost forgot. We found the charred remains of an exercise book in the fireplace of the Burgess house. I'm sorry, but what's left of it is unreadable. I wish I had better news, Mr. Prakash. You may never recover all your losses."

Mr. Prakash smiled. "Is not a problem."

"Why?" asked the constable.

"Because he has a duplicate book. Every night he copies all his sales into the other book – just in case," said Mrs. Prakash, who was listening.

"So, my loss is only from the Burgess account," added Mr. Prakash. "But now they won't steal from me or cause any more problems here."

Constable Ngata smiled. "All is well, then. Cheerio."

"Goodbye," said Mr. Prakash, "and thank you!"

Reggie Palmer arrived and waved at the constable as he climbed into his car.

Mr. Prakash walked up and both men silently watched through the window as the police car drove away. After a moment Reggie spoke. "How's the hand?"

Mr. Prakash raised his bandaged right hand and winced. "Burns are always painful."

Constable Ngata avoided the horses and slowly cruised away. He shook his head and grinned. He saw the bandage on Mr. Prakash's hand. He figured Reggie Palmer and Mr. Prakash, and perhaps some others, had set fire to the Burgess home. Small communities like this one frequently took matters into their own hands and, while it was dark, Mr. Prakash had probably spilled petrol on his hand before he lit a match. "Community justice," he said.

℗LUM ᴊAM

Chapter One

Hawkes Bay, 1964

The small rural township of Coleman lay nestled in low undulating hills, its distance from a substantial town enough to be either an inconvenience or a blessing. However, for most of its residents, its remoteness was favoured. Sheep dominated the outlying landscape and grazed contentedly on lush green pastures, and a few small herds of cattle provided additional income for farmers. Milking was out of the question, as Coleman was too far away for milk tankers to make deliveries.

The main highway into town wound through rugged bush-covered hills, across a narrow one-lane bridge, and then the road straightened into open rolling countryside. As a visitor, the first indication you were arriving in Coleman was the wind-battered and faded advertising board, announcing that the Geranium Tea Rooms were just five hundred yards ahead on the left.

A previous owner of the Tea Rooms had a passion for geraniums and planted colourful borders around the small parking area and along the front of the old colonial cottage, which had been converted into tea rooms about fifteen years previously. Sadly, the garden had been neglected and there wasn't a geranium to be seen now. Instead, purple, and white

68

agapanthus dominated what had once been a beautiful frontage. To the locals, the establishment was simply known as *The Geranium*.

The Geranium was popular with most local women. Various social clubs met there once a month, and some, like the Spinning and Crochet Club, even held regular weekly get-togethers. More frequently, many ladies would meet and chat informally about whatever was on their minds while sipping tea and nibbling on jam-and-cream-filled scones that they shouldn't really be eating.

Two women sat inside at a table that overlooked the parking lot, chatting amicably. As they always did when venturing out, both were well-dressed and took obvious pride in their appearance. Dorothy, an ex-teacher, had her auburn, shoulder-length hair done yesterday and wore a floral knee-length, belted summer dress, while her best friend, Bernice, was similarly attired, with the one difference that she was due for a *permanent* later in the week.

Suddenly, Dorothy sat a little straighter, patted her hair to ensure it was arranged as it should be, then reached out to her purse on the table and slid it a little closer. Bernice saw her friend's reaction and looked out of the window to find out the cause. A shiny, brand-new, and very expensive black Rover 95 pulled to a stop beside Dorothy's Anglia, and its two occupants gracefully alighted.

There was only one such vehicle in Coleman, and both Dorothy and Bernice were all too familiar with its owner, who just happened to be Dorothy's neighbour. They watched as Mrs. Helen Symanski and her friend Gloria Smith-Hewett strolled alongside the agapanthus towards The Geranium's entrance.

Dorothy gave Bernice a quick look of annoyance at the intrusion before holding up the mirror of her compact to inspect her lipstick. With a snap, she closed the lid and gave Bernice her full attention. "And we were having such a lovely morning," she said.

Bernice leaned forward slightly. "Did you know *she* was coming?"

Dorothy shook her head and frowned. "I had no idea."

"Why, good morning, Dorothy, Bernice. How lovely to see you both," said Helen as she entered the tea rooms and walked to the counter to place her order. Gloria dutifully followed and stood at Helen's side. She turned towards the two seated women and gave a small wave and a warm, friendly smile.

"How have you been, Helen? And how is Józef doing?" asked Dorothy, her own broad smile showing perfect white teeth.

"He doesn't stop complaining, you know how it is. Men act so tough until they get a small ailment, and then woe is me," she laughed, raising her eyebrows. "But he is better now. It was just the flu."

Dorothy and Bernice laughed politely as Helen placed an order for herself and Gloria.

With a furtive over-the-shoulder glance, Dorothy took the opportunity to give her a quick appraisal. Helen was attractive, and chic coordinated slacks and blouse combo emphasized her well-maintained figure. Her face was still free of wrinkles, which privately irked Dorothy.

When their order was taken, both women went to sit at an adjacent table.

"Please sit with us. We'd enjoy your company," offered Dorothy in the spirit of neighbourly friendship. She pulled out a chair, while Bernice slid another from under the table.

Predictably, both recent arrivals had ordered scones and tea and now sat comfortably, making small talk with Dorothy and Bernice.

"Are you excited about the A&P show?" Helen asked, her shoulder-length, jet-black hair bouncing with vitality.

Dorothy felt her heart rate increase slightly, and hoped no one noticed her agitation. "Yes, I think so. Is good for Coleman and gives the men something to do," she replied quickly, hoping the subject would change.

"And will you be entering the Preserves Competition again this year? I do enjoy it so." Helen smiled pleasantly and took a bite of her scone.

"I'm not sure about this year. I, uh, I may not enter," Dorothy stated.

Helen was delicately licking cream from her fingers. "All that cream and jam just goes to your hips."

Dorothy couldn't help herself. "So I've noticed." She innocently smoothed the front of her dress.

"So why won't you enter the competition? I find it so much fun," Helen pressed on, ignoring the barb.

Dorothy gave her friend Bernice a subtle look across the table. "We are having our house painted this year and Peter says I won't have time."

"How lovely… same yellow colour?"

"Is chardonnay, not yellow," snapped Dorothy a little more testily than she intended.

Helen smiled again before lifting her cup to her lips.

Chapter Two

Coleman was typical as far as country towns went. Residential homes, mostly colonial cottages with healthy established gardens, surrounded the downtown district. A few five-and ten-acre lifestyle blocks, mostly owned by retired or semi-retired couples, ringed the residential area, and beyond them lay the farms.

Dorothy and her husband of twenty years, Peter, lived on one of the five-acre lifestyle blocks. They grazed a few sheep, mostly for meat when they did a deal with the local butcher, and they maintained a healthy orchard that produced an extraordinary bounty of apples and plums. Why their orchard gave such an abundance of delicious sweet fruit, no one really knew. A local market gardener suggested it was just the right amount of sunshine, shelter, and water. He did add that someone knew what they were doing when they planted the orchard in the slight depression near the border fence of their neighbour and subsequently pruned it with a measure of skill as each tree produced an unusually high yield of exceptional-tasting fruit. This explanation suited Dorothy to a tee. Peter couldn't care less; the orchard came with the property when they purchased it six years ago, and he had little interest in growing fruit.

"And she asked if I would enter the Preserves Competition this year," said Dorothy with some indignance. She had just made Peter his lunch and he sat at their kitchen table finishing his sandwich as she stood near the sink, looking less than happy.

"Hmmmmm," replied Peter.

"That woman takes every opportunity to remind me how she has won the competition for seven straight years in a row. Seven!"

Peter put the remains of his sandwich back on the plate and turned to face her. "I don't know why you let Helen get to you. I like her. She and Joe are nice people, great neighbours and good friends."

"She's a cheat, and the only reason she wins is because she stoops to underhanded measures to ensure she is the reigning champion."

Peter laughed. "Oh, c'mon, now. Why would she do that?"

"To win and rub our noses in it!"

"It's a bloody jam making competition, for heaven's sake, not a rugby test."

Dorothy stepped closer to her husband. "My plums are the best in Coleman and that is undisputed."

"Yes, well..." Peter responded.

"And my jam tastes as good, if not better than hers. Even you've admitted that."

"But I'm not a jam referee."

"A judge. They're called judges, dear."

Peter shrugged.

"But her jam just has a better look, and a slightly richer colour that appeals to the judges. I can't duplicate that, and so help me, I've tried."

Peter wolfed down what remained of his sandwich, slid his chair back, and rose. "I must get to work."

Two afternoons a week Peter helped the local newspaper, *The Gazette*, as a type-setter. The extra income was useful. Additionally, he was a member of Coleman's Volunteer Fire Brigade. Occasionally, when there was need, usually a motor accident and seldom a fire, the siren would wind up and begin wailing loudly to notify all volunteers that they were urgently needed at the fire station. Often it happened at the most inopportune times, but Peter enjoyed the camaraderie and the feeling of being involved in the community.

Dorothy took his empty plate and began to wash the dishes. Peter stopped behind her and placed a hand on her shoulder. "Will you enter this year?"

"I'm tired of placing second to a cheat."

"Can you prove it?" he asked, raising an eyebrow in question.

She didn't look at him. "Well, no, but…"

"Then be careful with what you say, or your opinion may be seen as nothing more than jealousy and sour grapes."

Dorothy turned and dried her hands on a tea towel. "It's wrong that she cheats. It's the principle"

"Dot, let it go," Peter warned, using her pet name.

"But you wanted to paint the house."

"A storm is coming and we can paint after it passes." He looked out of the window and saw black clouds gathering in the distance. "I don't know why that jam competition is so important to you. It isn't like the prize is big. All you win is a bouquet of flowers and five quid. Seems hardly worth it."

"It's the ribbon, the blue ribbon – that's what I want."

Peter saw the determination on her face. He nodded. "If it makes you happy, enter the competition, and I wish you the best of luck. But if I were you, I'd pick the plums before the storm hits, or the ripe and best ones might be bruised from the wind."

Dorothy looked out of the window. "I will have to pick them later, when I return. I have to read to old Mrs. Wilson this afternoon." Once a week, on Wednesday afternoons, Dorothy visited a rest home, read a chapter from a book to one of the resident ladies, and chatted with her a while.

"Then enjoy," said Peter, grabbing his coat and heading towards the door.

A little while later, Dorothy stepped outside and climbed into her Anglia. Peering from behind the curtains next door, Helen watched Dorothy drive away towards the nearby retirement home.

A few drops of light rain began to fall as Helen walked out of her house, carrying a bucket. She wore a shawl over her hair, a raincoat, and gumboots. She passed by her own fruit-laden plum trees and headed towards their boundary fence.

Peter and Dorothy were good friends with Helen and Józef and socialized frequently. To make visiting each other easier, Peter had placed two large tree stumps, one on either side of the barbed wire fence, and draped an old car mat across the wire to make stepping over it possible without catching trousers or hands on the sharp barbs. Perhaps a gate would have been more convenient, but that task was assigned to Peter's rather long list of things to do and most likely he'd look at completing the job sometime next year, or perhaps even the year after.

Without pausing, Helen stepped easily across the wire onto a stump and strode confidently into Dorothy's orchard. With an expert eye she scanned the trees, looking for the best plums, and began to pick as rain started falling. She ignored blemished or damaged fruit and selected only the ripest, unmarked plums, placing each with considerable care in her bucket. The bucket was only half-full when she heard a car door close. She froze. *Dorothy or Peter must have returned home*, she thought with a measure of growing apprehension.

Helen had been inside Dorothy and Peter's home enough times to know that the orchard was visible from the kitchen window and that she needed to return home as quickly as possible or risk being caught.

She grabbed the bucket and ran for the fence. In her haste, she slipped on a wet wooden stump as she climbed over. Instinctively, she reached out to prevent herself from falling, and dislodged the car mat with her hand. It slid from the wire and folded on the ground, exposing the sharp barbed fence-wire. Her leg was already partly over the fence when it caught on a spike that ripped her trousers, scratching her thigh. She let out an involuntary cry as the bucket slipped from her grasp, scattering plums over the ground. Holding on to her hurt leg, she scooped up as many plums as possible before running towards her house as quickly as she could.

Mrs. Wilson was unwell, and the staff at the rest home thought it best for her and Dorothy to defer their visit. "Perhaps next week. She'll surely be better then," apologized the nurse with a frown.

Dorothy was quietly pleased. She could return home before the weather turned nasty, pick some plums, and devote the afternoon to making jam for her entry in the A&P show's Preserves Competition. She rushed home and, moments after stepping from her car, heard a muffled cry. Puzzled, she stopped to listen, but couldn't identify the sound or where it came from. She shrugged and entered her house to change her clothes and pick plums. It was already raining and she would need to hurry.

With her own bucket, Dorothy walked from her house, past the chook-pen, and towards the boundary fence and her delicious ripe plums. She saw it immediately; the car mat that normally hung across the barbed wire was now on the ground. As she bent down to pick it up and reposition it across the fence where it belonged, she saw a small pile of plums scattered beyond Helen and Józef's side of the fence. Her finely plucked eyebrows furrowed as she wondered how they ended up there. She shrugged, turned back towards her fruit trees, and immediately saw where the grass in her orchard had been trampled. Someone had recently been walking in there.

She looked over towards Helen's house but saw no one. *Kids?* she wondered. Ignoring the rain, she hooked the bucket onto a branch and began carefully searching for the premium plums. This was her year and she would win first prize if it killed her. She imagined the blue ribbon pinned on her dress as she began selecting and picking fruit.

She was cleaning the kitchen and Peter was back home from work, sitting at the table quietly reading the newspaper. Every now and then they heard a 'pop' as a lid sealed on one of the pots of jam that lined the counter. "There goes another," Peter said, teeth clamped around the stem of his pipe.

Dorothy smiled and reached across to feel the lids. "Two more to go."

"Whadda ya reckon, do you have the winning jam this year?"

Dorothy was bent down, peering intently at each jar, studying the texture and colour. "I've done my best, and to me these look perfect, but this will be the last competition I enter."

"Are you sure? And this is what you want?" Peter asked.

"Yes, I've done this long enough. Perhaps there is something else I can do at the A&P Show." She straightened and walked to the table, slid a chair back, and took a seat. "Do you think it was Helen that took the plums?"

A flash of lightning lit up the kitchen and thunder rolled in. They both looked outside through rain-splattered windows at the early evening sky.

"Nah, probably kids from down the road. I can't see a wealthy middle-aged woman creeping around stealing plums when she has all the money in the world to buy whatever she wants."

"Oh? Then you are out of touch," she laughed.

"Look, I can't see Joe supporting her doing that," Peter added, shaking his head. "He's a decent bloke. Nope, can't imagine him letting his wife steal the neighbours' plums." He grinned at her.

Another lid popped.

"One more," he added.

Dorothy leaned forward. "Winning the Preserves Competition is important to the women of Coleman... it's a status thing, and your skills are respected."

"OK, now tell me, how do you cheat making plum jam? Jam is jam, is just sugar and plums, right?" Peter queried.

"Oh no. Taste is obviously the most important thing, but there's more. Texture, colour, and presentation, these are all judged, and you could add thickeners and all sorts of other forbidden things to alter the consistency and colour..."

Even above the din of rain falling on the roof, the unmistakable sound of a siren winding up to pitch could be heard. Peter's smile disappeared. The siren was a signal to Coleman's volunteer fire brigade that lives or property were in danger. Something had happened. He made eye contact with Dorothy and was on his feet before the siren reached full tone.

"Be careful," she said as he rushed for the door, grabbing his coat.

Chapter Three

The Coleman Volunteer Fire Brigade boasted a single appliance. It was a three-year-old 1961 Dennis which was well maintained and loved. Every Christmas, with lights flashing, the fire-engine made a slow tour down Coleman's main street. For the kids, other than Santa Claus, this was the parade's highlight, especially when a waving fireman turned on the siren. However, tonight was not a festive occasion. A traveler had seen a car accident near the single lane bridge on Coleman's outskirts and reported the accident to the police. Constable Phil Strongbottom, the resident community police officer who was stationed in Coleman, contacted the New Zealand Fire Service and the Coleman fire brigade was duly alerted.

Within minutes of the wailing siren, vehicles sped through Coleman's streets towards the station and soon after, the Dennis was idling and waiting for the last volunteer fireman to arrive before heading off.

Constable Strongbottom was leading the small convoy in his black FC Holden with the bonnet mounted, emergency red light signaling the urgency as the Dennis appliance exited the station. Bringing up the rear was Tom, the butcher, in his old Bedford tow-truck that he used for hanging meat during a home kill job. Since it was an auto accident, the constable determined Tom should bring his truck as well. An ambulance had been called, but it would take thirty to forty minutes before it arrived as it was coming from a neighbouring, much larger town. With flashing lights and sirens, the procession headed south, past the Geranium Tea Rooms and towards the bridge. It still rained, but the downpour had eased somewhat, and the police car's wipers continued to work hard to clear the window of water as the constable rounded the last corner and saw that a vehicle had slammed into the bridge. With years of experience behind him, he assessed the situation and immediately knew what had happened.

Part of the bank alongside the highway had collapsed, spilling onto the road. The driver, heading northward towards Coleman, had rounded the corner, seen the small landslide and, to avoid the pile of dirt and rocks, braked hard, lost control, skidded, and slammed broadside into the bridge.

The fire-engine followed the police car around the corner and, by using its headlights, lit up the bridge and the car. Peter, in the front passenger seat of the fire engine, took in the scene and immediately recoiled. It was unmistakable. There was only one such car in Coleman and he doubted there were many others in the region. The black Rover 95 was in a sorry state and seemed to be seriously damaged. Who was driving, Helen or Józef? Were they both in the car?

The heavy rain had almost stopped and it was only drizzling lightly when Peter leapt from the cab of the Dennis. Another fireman was ahead of him, rushing for the car while Constable Strongbottom set up road cones.

Peter arrived at the Rover as the fireman ahead turned from the damaged automobile and vomited. He pushed past the retching firefighter and, lifting a torch, cautiously looked in through the smashed front window. The car contained only one male occupant, that much was obvious. It was Józef, Helen's husband. He lay face forward, unmoving, against the steering wheel into which he'd struck with some force. Blood was everywhere. Somehow, an artery must have been pierced or cut, as the entire front of

Joe's shirt was soaked bright red. There was too much blood, it was a mess, no one could survive such blood loss. Worst of all, they couldn't get near Józef to see if he was still alive.

Someone tried the doors; they were all stuck fast. Through impact, the Rover's chassis must have bent and the doors jammed.

"Aw geez, poor bugger," said the constable, looking through the window over Peter's shoulder. "Isn't that Jim, Joseph, uh, Sem–"

"Is Józef Symanski, my neighbour," replied Peter with a grimace.

"Yeah, the Hungarian chap. Nice missus," offered Phil Strongbottom. He scrunched his face. "What a bloody mess."

Peter sighed loudly as men came running up with tools to force the door open. "He's Polish, and a good bloke."

The constable moved out of the way to let the firemen do their job.

Peter was using a crowbar to pry the door open when suddenly, Józef groaned loudly.

"He's still alive!" someone yelled.

Other firemen had positioned crowbars around the door, and with a concerted timed shove, the door creaked and then sprung open.

Peter rushed to Józef's side. "Don't move, mate, we'll get you out of there."

Slowly, Józef moved and, by pushing himself away from the bent steering wheel, sat straight. He raised a hand to his forehead, which had been cut, and a small trickle of blood ran down his face. "oh, I, uh, must have been knocked out…"

"Don't move, keep still, Joe, moving will only make it worse. We need to stop the bleeding," warned Peter with growing alarm while he searched for the profusely bleeding wound on Józef's chest or abdomen.

The entire interior front of the Rover was splattered with red.

"What blood? Where's it coming from?" Józef asked, his face turning into a blood-smeared horrible mask of fear. He was dazed and attempted to step out of the car, but Peter held him firmly in place.

"Don't move until the ambulance arrives," Peter advised. "Try to relax, Joe."

A flood light had been assembled behind them. It lit the Rover's interior and the ground near the front door. The wetness Peter felt on his hands didn't feel like blood. He raised a hand to study it. It felt weird, and wasn't sticky or thick. He looked more closely and then licked it. It didn't taste like blood. "What is this stuff, Józef?

Józef groaned, slowly raised a hand to his left shirt pocket and felt inside. He carefully pulled out small shards of glass. "Shit!" he said.

Peter and the other watching firemen looked at each other in puzzlement.

"It's broken! Helen will be annoyed with me."

"What are you talking about?" Peter asked.

"Uh, food colouring. Helen asked me to go to the shop for food colouring and I put it in my shirt pocket. The bottle must have broken when I hit the steering wheel."

"Food colouring?" someone behind him questioned.

"Why drive all this way for food colouring? The shops in Coleman have it, I'm sure," Peter said.

Józef turned to look at him. "It was for her jam. She didn't want to buy it in Coleman in case someone saw." He rubbed his head and moaned again.

Peter stood. "Well, I'll be damned. The rain mixed with that food colouring looked gruesome." He bent down, "Józef?"

Józef looked up.

"Let me help you out."

Epilogue

The summer storm passed without further incident. The cut on Józef Symanski's head required a few stitches, and he was diagnosed with a severe concussion. His chest was sore, and he was fortunate he'd suffered nothing worse than a few bruised ribs. The hospital suggested he remain with them for a few days, but Józef adamantly refused and was released from hospital on the following day to the care of his wife. Everyone agreed that he was lucky and could have been much more seriously injured.

The following day, Dorothy's friend, Bernice, had been at the chemist shop and saw Helen limping as she carried a bag full of medication for Józef. She didn't stop to talk, and when asked about her injury, she claimed to be too busy for chit-chat because Józef needed her home and drove away with a roar in a borrowed Jaguar.

When Peter arrived home after rescuing Józef from the car accident and told Dorothy about the food colouring, she'd been speechless. She opened her mouth to offer some unsavory opinions, thought better of it, then got up and stomped around the house in a quiet rage.

"I owe you an apology, Dot. You were right, and I was wrong. I never would have believed it, and to think Józef knew and supported it, well, I never..." he shook his head.

"But will that woman have the gall to show up at the A&P show?

That's what I want to know," she replied once she had calmed down.

"Don't be too harsh on her. Is just a preserves competition, isn't like the future of the world depends on it."

Dorothy slowly turned, placed her hands on her hips, and glared at him.

The A&P show was being held in cooperation with the local school and with a farmer next door, who volunteered the use of his land and sheds. For the women of Coleman, the highlight of the two-day event was the preserves competition. As expected, and with the full support of her husband, Dorothy submitted her entry and, while she kept an eye open, Helen did not make an appearance, nor had she entered the contest. The results and prize-giving for the competition was one of the last stages of the event, held in the school hall that was full of spectators. Everyone came to see who would win.

After all that Dorothy had gone through, Peter decided that the least he could do was turn up in support of her. He leaned against the wall of the hall with his arms folded and, like everyone else, waited nervously.

Ian Morrison, the school headmaster, was one of the judges. The other was Juliet Cartwright, a typist at the council. Both had been judging the preserves competition for years and, by all accounts, had always done a superb job. Sadly, Headmaster Morrison loved the sound of his own voice and was a notoriously slow talker. He prattled on about the weather and the excellent quality of the preserves to be judged, and even managed to make a few announcements about upcoming school events. But eventually he came around to the matter at hand, which was what everyone wanted to know – who would win this year's contest?

He rose from his seat, gave Juliet a nod, and cleared his throat. "It brings me great joy to announce this year's winners of the preserves competition." He scanned the faces of the spectators in the school hall and continued, "Tony Sinclair, you'd better not be writing on the wall!"

Someone sniggered. The offending boy looked embarrassed and quickly exited the hall.

"C'mon, Ian, don't keep us waiting, we got things to do!" a spectator yelled.

Headmaster Morrison checked his notes. "Ah, yes… uh, third prize is being awarded to Harriet Goldman for her raspberry jam. Nice effort, Mrs. Goldman." He smiled, and Juliet held up a small bouquet of flowers and a yellow ribbon for the third-place winner to collect.

A polite round of applause filled the hall and Ian Morrison smiled. "Now then, the runner-up." He paused for a heartbeat or two for dramatic effect. "Second place is awarded to Bernice McClintock for her beetroot. Congratulations, Mrs. McClintock!"

Dorothy smiled. Bernice had never won anything in the competition before, and she was genuinely happy for her. She gave her a hug before Bernice walked to the table to receive her prize from Juliet.

When Bernice had collected her prize, Mr. Morrison adopted a solemn expression and again surveyed the gathering. "And now the moment we've all been waiting for… I must add, I do recall one of the first times I had the pleasure of judging this competition. It was in fifty-seven, or was it fifty-eig–"

"Mr. Morrison, please, my kids need to go to the toilet…!"

A few people laughed.

"Perhaps another time, eh? Yes, very well. And now for this year's winner of the preserves. First prize is awarded for her absolutely delicious gherkins to Mrs. – Jenny – Barstow!"

The audience responded with generous applause for the winner.

"Well done, Mrs. Barstow. Both Juliet and I were taken by your entry and your prize is thoroughly deserved," proclaimed Headmaster Morrison with a gracious bow of his head.

Dorothy looked down at her feet. Peter placed a consoling hand on her shoulder and whispered something in her ear. After a moment or two she looked up at him and smiled. "You wanted to show me the tractors?"

They both turned to leave.

"Uh, I have one last announcement," added Mr. Morrison.

A few people groaned, and those already walking for the exit stopped and curiously waited.

"Coleman's A&P Show organizing committee has come by some rather distressing news. In the spirit of fair and honest participation, the committee has decided to review some, er, results of past preserves competitions," Mr. Morrison smiled as he surveyed the audience. "Would Mrs. Dorothy Halbrook please step forward!"

Dorothy froze and then, after a moment, looked up at her husband.

"Go on, they called your name," he said, grinning.

A few people near Dorothy and Peter parted and created space for her.

She made her way to the stage in bewilderment, knowing it had something to do with Helen's cheating, but *what had the committee decided*? she wondered.

Principal Morrison waved her onto the stage, and she stood there self-consciously as he whispered something to Juliet before addressing the spectators.

"Upon my recommendation, the Coleman A&P Show organizing committee has supported my, er, *our* decision..." he turned to Juliet and gave an apologetic smile, "to reverse our judging results on several past preserves competitions. Congratulations, Mrs. Halbrook, you are indeed a winner. For the six years you entered your superb plum jam and were awarded runner-up, you should have won."

Dorothy couldn't contain her smile as he handed her an impressive bouquet of six blue ribbons sewn together.

"Additionally, the Coleman A&P Show organizing committee, would like to offer you the position of Preserves Judge for next year as Mrs. Cartwright will be unavailable."

Dorothy dabbed at a tear with a handkerchief. "I would love to."

Where the Wind Blows

Chapter One

Otago, 1968

The large, bay-coloured mare climbed the steep hill and onto a small ridge with ease. It paused briefly, and both the horse and its rider, Jock Marsh, a hill-country sheep musterer, looked up at the sunny face of a northwards-facing hill they still needed to climb, then beyond to the tops.

Jock reached up, lifted his wide-brimmed hat, and scratched his head. "Wanna give it a go, Rosie?" He spoke to his horse in a quiet, friendly tone, then affectionately patted her neck as the mare responded with a head toss and waited patiently for his command to proceed. Rosie was raised in the high country and knew every square mile and every track of the sheep-station, and had been on more musters than anyone could recall. She was strong and fast, a perfect stock-horse for him; he especially loved her peaceful demeanor.

His two sheepdogs, or *eye-dogs,* sniffed at something on the ground near a clump of tussock. Then one lifted a leg and relieved itself before moving to another tuft, a few yards away, to investigate another intriguing smell. "Bloody rabbits," said Jock.

He ignored the dogs; they were well-trained and he knew they wouldn't wander far. He twisted in the saddle and spared a quick look behind, and then another to each side as he scanned the desolate high country for mobs of sheep he may have missed and for a change in the weather. Only a few whispery clouds drifted beneath a deep blue sky, and for the next few hours at least, it would continue to remain calm and cool.

With a gentle squeeze of his legs, Rosie obeyed his command and moved towards the hill. Jock relaxed and allowed her to choose her own path upwards. With the reins held loosely, he held onto the pommel with one hand and gripped her mane with the other.

It was treacherous in the high country, but Jock trusted his horse with his life. The sure-footed animal knew the safest path, and all he needed to do was hang on. With tongues lolling, the two dogs scampered behind, finding their own way up. Jock didn't look back or down. Instead, he focused on where Rosie would walk and anticipated any quick lunges or sudden moves she would make that could easily throw him from the saddle.

The high country wasn't for the faint-hearted, and many a man had died up here. If you didn't end up in a rockslide or break your neck from a fall, then the weather could certainly kill you, but for Jock, this was home and there wasn't another place he'd rather be. Even the poofter paddock shepherds with their home-cooked meals and comfy beds were reluctant to leave the luxury of their lush, flat, green pastures and venture into the hills. Jock didn't care; he loved the solitude and quietness, and reveled in the majestic views of snow-capped mountains, deep gullies, and windswept tussock was what life was all about.

At the same time, his mate, Skinny, another hill-country shepherd, was mustering on the other side of the hill. When ready, the two of them would drive their combined mobs from the hills to the paddocks far below for shearing. Later that afternoon, he would meet Skinny at the shepherd's hut where they would have a good feed and spend the evening chatting while they continued mustering in this area.

Rosie finally crested the summit. An extensive area of moderately flat land lay ahead, while a razor-back ridge, about half a mile away, was too steep to climb and prevented him from ascending higher. Low-growing scrub, tussock, and a few large boulders were scattered haphazardly across the exposed plateau, and Jock knew he'd find more than a few sheep in the area. He dismounted, hung the reins over Rosie's neck so she wouldn't stand on them, and allowed her to forage while he stretched his legs and took a leak.

"Not much in the way of food," said Jock to himself as he completed his task, buttoned up and surveyed the ground, looking for fresh signs of sheep.

Alerted by something, one of his dogs began wagging its tail excitedly as it stared into the distance. Jock straightened and turned to see what drew the animal's attention. Sure enough, as he predicted, a small flock of sheep broke from cover and bolted. Jock gave a quick whistle and sent the dog away to head them off. He wanted the mob heading in a different direction, towards a trail that would eventually lead them down.

The other dog, tense with anticipation, moved to his side and whimpered, hoping to be noticed and called upon. The dog and Jock watched as the other sheepdog intercepted the small mob of twenty or so half-wild sheep and struggled to turn them. Jock cursed, then sent the second dog to help and, only too eager to please, the animal bounded enthusiastically away.

His dogs were experienced and instinctively knew what was required of them. Jock watched with a keen eye, occasionally assisting with a blow from his shepherd's whistle as the dogs asserted themselves and carefully swung the flock towards the trail where he would drive more sheep throughout the next day.

Rosie snorted and took a few agitated steps away. Puzzled, Jock turned from the sheep to see what startled her and found himself staring directly into the eyes of a wild horned ram. It was huge. Its wool was a dirty grey, charcoal colour mixed with brown, which blended perfectly with the large rocks where it had been hiding. No wonder he hadn't seen it when they arrived.

Immediately, Jock knew the ram wasn't feral, as this one didn't shed its wool. Its fleece was long and hadn't seen the clippers in some time. From the amount of wool it carried, Jock knew this ram had avoided muster more than once. It was a hermit ram, and he would have to drive it into the mob for shearing. Twigs and even some small branches were stuck in the dense filthy wool and poked outwards at oblique angles, making the animal appear more imposing and threatening. Impressive rounded horns, lethal weapons to the unwary, curved on each side of its head. Knowing it wasn't feral didn't make the situation better; he knew some aggressive rams could cause serious injury and even kill, so he needed to be careful.

He quickly turned towards Rosie, but she trotted off to a safe distance and now stared, her ears pricked forward, at the unexpected interloper with some concern.

A hermit ram could pose a serious threat to a man, as generally they carried less fat and were more muscular than normal pasture rams. To survive in hostile country, animals needed to be in good health, or they'd die. He knew he should not underestimate the ram, as it could be dangerous.

Through overgrown wool covering most of its eyes, the hermit ram stared at Jock, its nostrils flaring. He sensed the animal wasn't afraid of him. The problem was, Rosie was too far away, and he couldn't access his .303 calibre Lee Enfield rifle, which was securely strapped to the saddle. Any time he encountered an aggressive ram, he would cull it immediately, but at the moment, his rifle was out of reach.

Slowly, he began to step backwards, and the ram, emboldened, took a step forward and then another, following him. Jock stopped, risked a quick look at his dogs, and whistled loudly for them to return. He saw the ram's breathing quicken and knew it would attack.

"BUGGER OFF!" he yelled and leapt in the air, waving his arms, hoping to frighten it. "HUUUAAAAAAA!"

The ram wasn't impressed. It lowered its head and charged.

Jock played rugby and enjoyed the position of flanker. He was a decent-sized bloke, bigger than many, and strong. He'd tackled many a massive forward in his days and never shied away from physical contact. When the ram charged, he immediately bent his knees, crouched a little, and faced the oncoming beast as if playing a game of rugby. However, this was no rushing forward or second rower; this was an angered, wild hermit ram intent on harming him. He waited until the last second, then dove to the side, falling onto a shoulder, rolling over and springing to his feet in a smooth, well-practiced motion. He could almost taste the ram's earthy smell and filth as it flew past, dags rattling. His dogs were fast approaching, but still too far away to assist.

The ram turned, took a moment to prepare and, with its head down, sprung forward. Jock was ready and waiting. All he needed to do was buy time for the dogs to arrive and distract the ram so he could retrieve his rifle. However, the ram had other plans.

Again, Jock bent his knees and partially crouched as the ram bore down on him. Just as before, he intended to dive to the side, but his foot caught on a protruding rock and he stumbled. Before he could regain his balance and dive away, the ram drove into his leg.

Chapter Two

The sound of barking dogs was the first thing Jock heard when he came to. That was unusual in itself, as his dogs were *eye dogs* that stared at sheep, not *gravel-scrapers* that barked, with little to no effect. But they were yapping nonetheless, and despite the mental fog and the growing awareness of pain in his leg, he was pissed off.

A groan escaped his lips as consciousness fully returned. "Geezus," he gasped, and simultaneously grabbed his leg and risked a quick look at the ram. It had moved and now stood some distance away, feigning only mild irritation at the bothersome dogs. It chewed nonchalantly on some tussock and, for time being, appeared to have lost interest in him. Jock was relieved and looked down at his leg and knew it was broken. It hurt like hell.

He lay down, breathing hard, and tried to control the shooting pain that speared his leg and blossomed outwards, turning into pure agony. With eyes tightly closed, Jock tried to focus his thoughts. It was difficult as the pain came in waves, each successive one more severe than the last. The relief came in a narrowing and lengthening tunnel of blackness.

The quietness hung over him like a shroud. He blinked his eyes open and stared at the late afternoon sky, realizing that he was in trouble. Where earlier a few small white wisps drifted aimlessly across the blue expanse, grey clouds now gathered and dominated the sky. The weather was changing. He breathed in small, quick gasps, and tried to raise himself into a sitting position. The movement jarred his leg and he screamed. With watery eyes and clenched teeth, he persisted and, with some difficulty, sat upright.

Rosie was grazing about a hundred yards from where he lay; she may as well have been a hundred miles away. Both dogs lay near and watched him; they sensed something wasn't right and appeared unsettled. He called for his horse, but through his pain, it sounded like 'Hosie'. She looked up briefly and then resumed her foraging. He called to her again, and this time she didn't respond at all.

He looked around for a stick or something to use as a splint, but up here in the hills, trees were a scarcity. His immediate concern was for the changing weather. A nor'westerly was driving in distinctive *arch* shape clouds, and that was worrying – it would rain, temperatures would plummet, and where he now sat, he was completely exposed.

A cluster of boulders and one large rock with an almost vertical sheer side lay about twenty yards away and could provide some protection from wind and rain when conditions deteriorated. *But how to get there*? he thought, as the reality of his precarious situation settled on him. He knew, perhaps better than most, how dangerous the high country could be. When you work the tops, the weather is always a worry, he'd tell people. Right now, he had to survive the night, and he knew that would prove to be a challenge.

He awkwardly removed his swanni, placed it under his leg, and wrapped it around as tightly as he could. The pain was excruciating, and he cried out and began to feel light-headed again, but after a few quick, deep breaths, the dizziness passed. The two dogs didn't wander and stayed close, watching anxiously.

With his sleeve, he wiped the sweat from his brow, then reached for his discarded hat, placed it securely on his head, and took a deep calming breath. By using his arms and uninjured leg to push, he began to drag himself slowly towards the rocks. The swanni protected his leg a little, but the agony was intense, and every movement caused shooting pains so severe that he almost gave up. If he couldn't make it to the shelter, he wondered if he would even survive the night. He shook his head to rid himself of the doubt, slid his body a few more inches, took a breather, and kept going.

Time seemed to stop for Jock. The pain was unbearable, and every move he made jolted his leg so that the hurt erupted outwards. At times he yelled in agony, other times he screamed in defiance as he pushed on – inch by inch – foot by foot. His clothes were damp from sweat, and he knew they needed to dry before darkness descended or he'd begin to shiver and risk exposure. He looked over his shoulder for the umpteenth time and was reassured by the rock's closeness.

Encouraged by his progress, he pushed on. Luckily, the ground was reasonably flat, which made it easier, but any indentation, bump, or unevenness in the terrain he dragged himself over caused him to cry out. At times he felt so lightheaded, he thought he'd pass out from pain. Thankfully, the sensation passed.

Both dogs suddenly sat up and turned away to look at something. Jock paused to see what held their interest. Partly obscured by a boulder, the ram appeared. It stared malevolently, challenging, and stood proudly arrogant. Sadly, he knew that if the ram was close, Rosie would stay away, and that was a problem. He looked around but couldn't see her anywhere. He tried calling – nothing.

He considered sending the dogs to chase the ram away but reluctantly decided against it, as he didn't want to provoke and annoy it any further. If the ram decided to charge, he would not be able to protect himself. However, if the ram kept its distance and did nothing more than watch, he could live with that. If it came any closer, however, Jock decided he'd send both dogs after it and hope for the best.

With his jaw tightly clenched, Jock continued to drag himself to the group of boulders. He was thirsty and hoped some water from recent rains had pooled in the rocks so that he could have a drink.

It took an age, but with agonizing slowness, he finally made it. He sat with his back against a towering boulder, exhausted and breathing hard. Near where he sat, a small pool of water collected in a slight depression in a rock, and with some difficulty, he could twist and lower his head to drink. There wasn't much water and he decided to leave some for later. He'd need it if it didn't rain. The dogs would find water on their own and he wasn't worried about them at all.

Sitting against the boulder offered some security. It lessened the chance of the ram attacking, and there was some protection from the weather, but signaling for help or building a fire was out of the question. He had matches, but nothing to burn except clothes and a few handfuls of dried tussock grass.

As Jock rested, he knew he needed to evaluate his situation. The only useful things he had were a sharp knife, matches, a packet of tobacco, which had no practical use, and a shepherd's whistle that hung from around his neck. There was no point in trying to signal Skinny for help, he was too far away and be wouldn't be missed until later. His mate, Skinny, wouldn't suspect anything was wrong until it was completely dark, and the sun, hidden behind grey clouds, was only now beginning to set. What bothered him the most was the weather. It had become colder and he shivered.

He carefully untied his swanni, and another involuntary yell escaped his lips as he accidentally moved his broken leg. Startled by the sudden pain, he jerked his head backwards and hit it on the rock behind. He cursed. After a few moments, he reached up and pulled the thick swanni down over his head, feeling warmer at once.

When the pain in his leg settled to a persistent throb again, he decided to gather as much tussock as he had within reach. Problem was, the tussock would burn quickly and wouldn't provide any lasting heat that would benefit him. Alternatively, he could stuff it in his swanni for insulation to help him keep warm.

"Rosie, Rosie!" he yelled.

It was growing dark, and he couldn't see much at all.

The solitude was complete, the silence heavy. Nothing stirred or moved but the tussock grass, disturbed by a gentle soft wind.

Chapter Three

Skinny gave the mutton stew another good stir. It had been ready for some time, and he was hungry and impatient for Jock to arrive so they could eat. They always ate together and talked about their day before turning in for the night. He replaced the lid, pulled the pot from the flames, and put it on the bench. It was done cooking.

With a heavy sigh, he walked to the door and went outside to check if Jock was riding up, but as it was already night, there wasn't anything to see; it was just black. He shivered. It was chilly. *Be another cold evening,* he thought. With no sign of his mate, he looked up at the starless sky. "Bloody rain," he said, before returning to the warmth inside.

His mother was the only person alive who called him Bartholomew. To everyone else, he was 'Skinny', an inaccurate moniker given to him by a school rugby coach who insisted the teenager eat less and pretend to be thin. It was intended to be motivational for the young man. It didn't work. Skinny kept growing both in height and weight and, much to the surprise of his coach, he became a force to be reckoned with on the rugby paddock. As a *prop*, the only things that stopped him were knocks to the head and the multiple concussions that followed. His family doctor warned him that if he continued to play rugby and hurt his noggin, it would cause permanent damage. Poor Skinny was heartbroken. Rumours were abundant that a provincial team had been looking closely at him, but with the doctor's and his mum's stern warnings still ringing in his ears, Skinny hung up his boots.

That was when he met Jock Marsh. Jocko had taken him under his wing and taught him everything he needed to know about mustering sheep, and Skinny had taken to it with the same skill he displayed on the rugby field. The hard work kept his weight manageable, but he also needed a sizeable, strong horse to carry him and plenty of food to keep him fed and content.

Skinny stared at the pot of mutton stew and felt his stomach rumble. Should he…? *Perhaps one small plate, just to take the edge off,* he thought. But he couldn't, and even thinking about it, he felt guilty. Up here in the hut, they never ate alone and always waited for everyone to arrive before starting the meal. He stoked the fire impatiently. *Where the bloody hell is Jocko?*

Jock was never this late. Something wasn't right; Skinny felt it deep inside and knew his mate was in trouble. Sometimes either one of them was delayed for a short time, but both nearly always arrived at the hut before it was completely dark. He pulled on his swanni and stepped outside again. The wind had picked up a notch, and with it, the temperature fell. With no stars or moon, it was pitch black. He stopped to listen for a gunshot or whistle that would signal Jock needed help.

The shepherds' hut was situated just beneath the summit of a hill, in a slight depression that was littered with scree. The hut wasn't fancy, it was basic. It had bunks for four, a fireplace with a chimney, and a kitchen counter. Outside, against the wall, a small tub was used for washing dishes and for other, more personal tasks. The hut was sparse and functional, but after a tough day mustering, it was homey and welcoming.

Skinny retrieved his horse, which was hobbled not far away, led it back to the hut, and began to saddle it, preparing to venture out. What he was doing was considered dangerous, as only a fool would ride in the high country when it was pitch-black.

With his horse saddled and ready, Skinny returned inside and quickly wolfed down a few spoonfuls of mutton stew. He grabbed his oilskin coat, his rifle, also a Lee Enfield .303, some food he placed in his saddlebag, and a torch. There was no paper or pencil to leave a note, so he couldn't leave a message. He ate a couple more mouthfuls of his dinner, closed the door, released both his dogs from their chains, and mounted his horse.

"Alrighty, where are ya, Jocko?" Skinny muttered as he urged his horse towards the summit where he'd ride down the other side and begin to search.

A few drops of rain splattered Skinny's back as he gently pulled his horse to a stop. Somewhere beneath him was Jocko. "JOCK!" he yelled once, and then again. He waited for a reply but heard nothing. No answering cry, no response, no signaling whistle or gunshot.

He was genuinely concerned and felt his heart beat faster. "JOCKO!"

His voice, carried by the wind at his back, dissipated in the cold high country air, lost amongst miles and miles of tussock and a harsh, craggy landscape.

He listened and waited.

He turned slightly. "JOCKO!" he yelled again and cocked his head to better hear an answering cry or signal.

He heard it then. Was it the sound of a footstep on rock? "JOCKO?" Nothing. Was he mistaken?

His horse shifted position while both his dogs stood obediently nearby. Extracting the torch from his pocket, he shone it at the dogs. First one, then the other, turned their heads, and their ears pricked forward. There was something.

"JOOCCKKOO!"

There it was again, the same sound, and this time closer. He shone his torch into the black void and saw only rain, but this time he could identify the noise. It was the distinctive sound of a horse's footfalls dislodging stones; it was unmistakable, and Skinny felt immediate relief.

Again, he shone his torch into the blackness and saw two reflective eyes staring back at him. A horse but no rider. It was Rosie. "Where's Jocko, girl?" he asked. His voice was thick with worry.

He dismounted and walked to the approaching mare. At once, he saw the reins were draped over her neck and looped over the pommel. Jock hadn't fallen; he'd placed the reins there. He stroked Rosie's neck and looked for a clue that could tell him where she'd been and what happened.

Jock's oilskin was still secured to the saddle, as was his rifle and a few other odds and sods. "Shit!" He turned to stare out into the vastness. "Where are ya, mate?"

He checked Rosie for any sign of injury, and after looking at all her feet, he still found nothing. She was healthy and fine. *What the hell happened*? he thought. Skinny knew that without a coat or food, Jock was in a whole heap of trouble.

The rain turned into a light drizzle, nothing serious or of any real concern unless you were hurt and had no shelter. A dozen questions came to mind, and Skinny pondered each carefully as he considered what he should do.

The harsh reality was chilling. It was most probable Jocko was injured and needed help, but how bad was it and what shape was he in? Skinny knew one thing for certain, if Jocko were alive, he would blow his damn whistle. As for Rosie, it was common for horses to return home or to the nearest hut. He knew of drovers that deliberately let their horses find their own way back while they caught a lift home in a bus or car.

He walked back to his horse and extracted a length of rope. He tied one end to Rosie's bridle and the other to a metal loop on his saddle. She had no choice but to follow. He stroked her neck again. "Where's bloody Jocko, girl?"

Stock horses were familiar with the sound of gunfire, but up here, he couldn't take a risk that the animals wouldn't balk at the sound. Not far away, there was an old fence line, and he could securely tether the horses to a post while he fired a signal shot. He mounted his roan gelding and guided him down, allowing him to walk at his own pace, safely navigating around obstacles and hidden dangers.

The fence he sought loomed from the darkness. Lit by his torch, drops of water hung tenuously from rusty wire for a brief moment, then blew away as the wind increased. Wrapped comfortably in his oilskin coat, Skinny tied each horse to a sturdy lichen-covered post, then untied his rifle, removed its protective cover, and clicked the five-shot magazine into place. With his torch illuminating the way, Skinny walked a short distance, stood behind a boulder, and worked the bolt, loading a round into the breech. With the butt firmly against his shoulder, he pulled the trigger and felt the recoil as the firearm discharged. The violent explosion of sound thundered across the hills.

He inclined his head and listened.

Chapter Four

Even in the moisture-filled air, the distinct sound rattled over tussock and echoed repeatedly. Jock's eyes snapped open. Even though he was exhausted, he couldn't sleep. The constant throbbing, incessant pain, rain, and biting cold prevented that. His dogs stirred and raised their heads at the unexpected noise. These dogs were not pets; they were working animals, unused to the affection and privilege of lying at his side. Their combined warmth helped him a little, but he was still very cold.

Despite his discomfort and agony, he managed a smile and nod. "Good on ya, Skinny," he croaked. He reached beneath his swanni, grasped the flat shepherd's whistle, and placed the familiar folded metal instrument in his mouth. He clamped down onto it with chattering teeth, inhaled, and blew a long, hard, piercing blast. The shrill sound cut through the night and rain, but would it be loud enough for Skinny to hear? The unfamiliar signal caused the dogs some anxiousness, and they rose and began pacing nervously. After a few moments, he blew again, then again. The dogs watched him, uncertain as to what they should do.

The hermit ram stood a short distance away with its back against a rock where it sought shelter from the rain. It raised its head at the sound and sniffed the air, then took a tentative step closer.

He was wet, his trousers were soaked, and he could feel dampness at his back where he leaned against the rock. But his chest was mostly dry, and with the heat of both dogs, it kept him from freezing. He had hope. However, he knew Skinny would have difficulty finding him while it was dark. All he could do was continue to blow the whistle, and with some luck, Skinny could tell from which direction the sound came. It would be a long and miserable night, and he wished dawn would come. He blew his whistle again and continued doing so every five minutes.

Before Skinny had returned the rifle back to its cover, he thought he heard an answering whistle. It was distant, but the wind was most likely blowing the sound away. If that was so, he reasoned, Jocko couldn't be far. With his two dogs and Rosie following, Skinny let his horse find its own way down.

The sound of the whistle became fainter and Skinny believed they were riding away from Jock. With a little guidance, he angled his horse in a different direction, and again, a few minutes later he heard the shrill tone, this time a tad louder. Occasionally, there were no repetitive signaling whistles. During those times, Skinny dismounted, blew his own whistle and waited until Jock's whistling resumed, then continued down, slowly, through the inky darkness.

As the night progressed, Skinny zig-zagged across the hills, heading west, then east, and finally south. When he kept pursuing a southerly route, the whistling grew noticeably clearer.

In the east, the sky was lighter. The grey of a new morning seeped across a leaden sky, and Skinny was relieved, although he hadn't heard a blast from Jock's whistle in at least an hour. He blew on his own whistle a few times but heard no answering call. Skinny was scared and hoped Jock was only sleeping.

As dawn broke, Skinny rode as quickly as he dared. Still, he hadn't heard Jock's whistle. He knew of a plateau not far away and was heading towards it to try to wake his friend with another gunshot.

While Skinny may have suffered from some nasty knocks to the old block playing rugby and suffered double vision for a while, it hadn't permanently dulled his senses. His vision was keen again. As he descended onto the plateau, he immediately saw movement in his peripheral vision and spotted a monstrous, filthy ram near an outcropping of large boulders. The animal was behaving oddly as it faced a large rock with a sheer side that was partly obscured. It was erratically tossing its head and appeared agitated. Then it saw him and turned to face the new, unwelcome threat. Skinny was immediately alert to the danger and wondered if this creature had anything to do with Jock's disappearance. He had to investigate. Without dismounting, he reached for the rifle, pulled it from its cover, and clicked in the magazine before sliding from the saddle.

Unafraid, with its head held high, the ram focused its attention on him and began to advance in his direction. Skinny wasn't surprised when Jocko's two dogs ran out from behind the big rock. He felt immediate relief. *Jocko is here*, was his first thought. *And that bloody ram has something to do with it,* was his second.

"Jocko?" he yelled.

There was no reply.

If Jock's dogs were here, so was Jock. *Why aren't you answering me?*

But first, he had to deal with the darn ram that was sizing him up. "You're a bad-tempered mongrel, aren't ya?" he said quietly as he took

111

a few steps away from the horses and calmly dropped to a knee. "Did ya nail, Jocko?"

The ram began to run. Sticks and small branches that poked from its wool jerked and shook wildly as the beast bore down on Skinny.

He calmly raised the rifle and carefully lined up the front and rear sights. A horse snorted in fear and quickly moved away. His own dogs were nervously pacing behind him and watched the approaching ram with some anxiety.

The ram lowered its head and charged. Skinny held off, waited patiently for the right moment, then slowly exhaled and squeezed the trigger.

Click. Then the ram struck him in the chest and sent him sprawling, flat on his back, knocking his rifle away. In his excitement, he'd forgotten to chamber a round.

He lay winded and tried to regain his breath as the ram turned and took another aggressive step closer. With his lungs heaving for air, Skinny rolled away, trying to buy time to regain his breath and strength. He could smell it, taste it. The animal stank.

Still out of breath and very near panic, he reached for the .303 as the ram pawed at the ground; he knew it would charge again in a matter of seconds. Still breathless and flat on his back, he fumbled for the bolt and managed to load a shell. The ram stopped its pawing and lowered its head. With the Lee-Enfield held in one shaky hand, Skinny reached out at the same time as the ram sprung forward. At point blank range, he pulled the trigger and rolled away. The explosion of sound was loud; the horses jerked their heads and trotted a few yards aside.

The ram's momentum carried it forward a foot or two before its lifeless body slid to a stop where only moments ago he had been. Skinny lay unmoving. His chest rose and fell heavily as he tried to recover. The ram wouldn't cause any more problems; it was dead. Slowly, with a grunt and a curse, Skinny rolled onto his knees and tentatively pushed himself up and rubbed his chest. It hurt but didn't feel like there was any permanent damage. He spared the carcass a swift look and, as quickly as he could, walked to where the dogs had appeared from.

"Jock!" he cried, seeing his mate propped up against the large boulder, his eyes closed.

He was unconscious, and Skinny knew Jock was near death and probably suffering from severe exposure. Hypothermia, or exposure, as it was locally called, was caused when the body lost warmth faster than it could generate heat. But Skinny knew something else had happened, and needed to know why Jock was here in the first place.

His own chest still hurt, but nothing more serious than a bad bruise that would turn an ugly blue. He'd suffered worse playing rugby, but failing to load his rifle was a dangerous mistake, one he'd never forget.

Careful not to touch or move his friend, Skinny searched for blood or signs of an injury, but couldn't see anything after a quick look. Jock's breathing was shallow, and when Skinny cautiously touched his face with the back of his hand, it felt cold. He removed his coat, draped it over his friend, ran back to the horses, led them closer to the rocks, and hobbled them both. He removed Jock's oilskin coat from his saddle and placed that over him as well. Now he needed to hurry and find something to burn. He ran to some nearby scrub, pulled at its branches, and after a minute or two, he gathered an armful of kindling and brought it to the rocks near Jock. It was difficult to light the fire, but eventually, flames took hold, and he ran off to find more wood.

Within a short time, a thick column of smoke billowed upwards, caught the wind, and disappeared in a southerly direction. The blazing fire began to radiate some heat.

Skinny knelt beside his friend. "Jocko, can ya hear me? Wake up, c'mon, mate, wake up, talk to me."

Jock stirred.

"Jocko!" Skinny pleaded. "Wake your bloody arse up!"

Jocko moved his head and groaned loudly.

"Shit," exclaimed Skinny as he realized that Jocko was in severe pain. He couldn't see why and didn't want to move him to find out. "Wake up, mate. Jocko, Jocko!"

Jocko's eyes blinked open and he groaned again. "S-Skinny," he managed to croak. "We g-gotta finish the muster." He began to shake, and his teeth chattered.

Skinny knew Jock's mind was elsewhere; one of the effects of exposure. "What happened, mate? Tell me. Where does it hurt?"

With chattering teeth, Jock looked up at his friend as his mind slowly returned to the present. "I knew you'd c-come. What took you so b-bloody long?" He swallowed. "B-Busted me right l-leg… the ram g-got me." With the realization the aggressive ram could be close, he turned to look past Skinny.

Knowing it was safe to do so, Skinny placed a reassuring hand on his shoulder. "Is alright, I got him, he won't bother us anymore. But now I gotta get you warm and out of here."

"I'm s-so c-cold."

Skinny rose. "I'll get more scrub."

The heat from the fire was intense. The rocks around where Jock lay radiated the heat, but still, he shivered uncontrollably beneath two oilskin coats. With the absence of trees, Jock's rifle was the only option to use as a main splint and Skinny placed it on the ground along the outside of his broken leg. On the inside, he had a short, relatively straight branch from some scrub that he would use as a second splint. There wasn't anything else he could use, and it would have to do until he could find something better. He had rope; the unpleasant and painful task of strapping Jock's leg lay before them both.

"It might hurt a bit," suggested Skinny as he scooted into a better position.

"Ya d-don't say."

"Don't be a bloody ponce – be over in a tick and we can walk out of here, eh?" With surprising gentleness, Skinny threaded the rope beneath Jock's leg, around the rifle, and back over to the branch. With both hands flat on the ground on either side of him, Jock tensed as Skinny pulled the rope tighter.

Jock let out a long whoosh as he felt the pain shoot up his leg.

Around and around, Skinny threaded the rope and tightened it as much as he dared. Jock screamed and, in reflex, lifted his torso up from the ground, leaning on his hands in agony.

"Got any beers in your saddlebags?" Skinny asked, trying to distract him as he finished tying the rope.

"B-Bugger off... aaaagggghhhhhhh!"

Skinny winced. He knew it was painful, but he had no option.

What they hadn't talked about was how to get out of here. No vehicle could drive this far up, and the only way to get home was to ride.

Skinny noticed how Jock's shivering had decreased noticeably, which was a good sign. The fire was hot, and every now and then he would run off, tear another bush apart, and return with a load of wood to burn.

"So, how we gonna do this, Skinny? What did ya have in mind?"

"What do ya mean?"

"Getting me down. I hope you got a plan, cause I don't."

Skinny was silent as he considered his reply. After a dozen heartbeats he said, "Unless I leave you to get help, you're gonna have to ride, mate. No other way."

Now it was Jock's turn to remain silent. He took a deep breath and exhaled slowly. "Yeah."

Jock sat against the rock and tried to move into a better position. Since Skinny had departed to bring help, he'd been left alone with his two dogs and the wind. He'd had time to think and reflect a little, and cursed himself for his stupidity at dismounting his horse before thoroughly making sure it was safe to do so. He should have, at least, held on to Rosie's reins.

The splint helped a lot and kept his leg from moving and aggravating the break, but now he had to wait for Skinny to return.

Before he left, Skinny made sure there was a large pile of scrub to burn. It wouldn't last during the entire night when he'd need it the most. He had his coat, rifle, and what little food Skinny had brought with him. As they'd already been doing, the dogs would have to fend for themselves. They were tough and could handle it.

The solitude affected him the most. Normally he loved being up here, alone in the high country. But then, normally he had the freedom to move around and return home whenever he chose. He sighed.

Up here, nearly everything constantly changed, especially the weather. One element was unwavering – the wind. Its presence was familiar, comforting. It spoke in hushed whispers, the tones varying as its strength increased or decreased. At night the wind could be angry, and its biting chill spoke warnings of danger. During the day, its freshness made you feel alive and was invigorating. Even now, as he listened, the wind blew over the rocks, through the tussock, hissing ever so slightly. The wind had helped Skinny find him.

The sky darkened, and Jock ate the last of the food Skinny left for him. He was still hungry, but not starving. A good hot meal would be nice, he thought wistfully. Like the previous night, clouds gathered, and it would probably rain again. He didn't remember much about last evening other than being cold and wreaked in pain. Since his leg was now immobile for the most part, the shooting pains had stopped. It still throbbed, but he could shift his position slightly without much discomfort, and that offered some relief.

But the rain and cold frightened him a little. Not being able to take care of himself was tough, and no matter what, he had to ride it out patiently – one last night, and then Skinny would return with assistance. Now he had two oilskin coats and could light a fire when he needed to, and that would help. On Skinny's advice, he kept some brush tucked under his swanni to keep dry and make lighting a fire easier.

The first drops of rain began to fall, and Jock repositioned his oilskin coat a little. He was exhausted and felt a little insecure. He called for his dogs and had them lie down beside him, and their warmth and presence made him feel a little better.

Good ol' Skinny. If not for him, he'd be dead. Jack stared upwards into the blackness and hoped Skinny would return soon. After tonight, he doubted he would survive another twenty-four hours in the cold and wet – he felt fragile and uncharacteristically a little lonely. He blinked away a tear, closed his eyes, and listened to the wind as it blew across the high country he loved so much.

Epilogue

"You have a visitor, Jock," said the nurse with a smile as she stepped aside and made room for the big man. Skinny entered the ward and loomed large at the foot of the bed, beaming from ear to ear.

The nurse's crisp uniform swished as she walked away.

"She's a bit of alright," Skinny said when he knew she couldn't overhear him.

Jock eased himself into a more comfortable position and returned the smile. "So many nurses and so little time."

Skinny grinned. "Is good to see you, mate. You had us all worried there for a bit. It was quite journey back down."

"I don't remember much, and I don't remember when you came back for me. Just some memories of my leg hurting as you brought me back down. I owe you a lot."

"Nah, you don't owe me a thing, except a beer and maybe a new coat. Mine stinks of piss." He laughed and then his face turned serious. "We nearly lost you, you know. That last night was the coldest it had been up there in a while, and how you kept alive beats me." He shook his head in wonder.

"I woke shivering and lit the fire. That made the difference."

Skinny looked at the cast on Jock's leg. "The nurse told me it was a bad break."

"Yeah, but they said I would heal and be as good as new in a couple of months."

Skinny nodded. "Good. We miss ya. Uh, you know we took the ram carcass back with us?"

Jock shook his head. "Nope, didn't know that."

Skinny lifted his swanni and singlet to reveal a blue, black and yellow coloured bruise on his chest. "You know the bastard got me too!"

Jock laughed. "How did ya manage that souvenir?"

"I'll tell you about it one day." He wanted to change the subject and walked to the side of the bed and slowly eased himself into a chair. "Do you remember that a year or two ago, Murray skited how he shot a monstrous hermit ram? He claimed it attacked his horse and was the meanest and ugliest mongrel he ever saw."

Jock nodded. "I do. Didn't he say how after he shot it, it just ran away?"

"He called it the 'devil ram'," Skinny laughed.

"It was a story he made up, nothing in it," Jock said.

"Muzza claimed he shot it between the eyes, and the ram just shook its head and took off," said Skinny. "Shooting it did nothing more than piss it off."

Jock smiled. "Another of Muzza's bullshit stories."

"The ram that attacked you had a huge hunk of its right horn missing, near the crown at the base by its skull. Is unmistakable that a bullet did the damage. We think it was the same ram Muzza bragged about, and it would've attacked you and Rosie if it got close enough. It wasn't afraid of man or horse," Skinny added. "You were bloody lucky."

"You're pulling my leg!" Jock scoffed and shook his head in disbelief.

"We kept the head as a trophy, a memento for you when you're up and about again."

Jock grimaced and then laughed.

GANGWAY TO WAR

Twelve thousand brave New Zealanders
lost their lives fighting for their country
during WWII; our losses were the
highest in the commonwealth. On a per-
capita basis, one in every one-hundred-
and-fifty New Zealanders died.

Chapter One

1940 Wairarapa

Kevin studied himself in the mirror and slightly turned his head, first to the left, then to the right. Eminently pleased, he reached for the red-labelled jar of Brylcreem, unscrewed the lid, dug two fingers into the white goop, and began to rub it into his palm to warm and soften it slightly. After a few seconds, he began to massage the oily cream into his damp hair and scalp with both hands. He didn't need much, as his hair was short and tidy. "By Jove, some chaps are lucky," he said with a soft voice, repeating the Brylcreem advertising slogan as he checked to make sure he hadn't missed any spots.

With his comb, he carefully began to style his coiffure and pat any wayward strands into place. Unhappy with his first attempt, he began again, and eventually, his brilliant, shiny hair sat and looked exactly as he wanted. He completed his grooming with a wink, then thoroughly washed the comb and slid it carefully into the back pocket of his trousers before stepping back from the mirror for another critical self-appraisal.

Eighteen-year-old Kevin Hargreaves wasn't vain and seldom applied any pomade to his hair. There wasn't much use for it on a farm, and anyway, the oily stuff only stained his hat. However, tonight was different. He was going to a dance at the local hall and he wanted to look his very best.

"Well, if it isn't Clark Gable himself," said Mr. Hargreaves as Kevin stepped self-consciously into the kitchen.

"I think he looks very handsome," said his mother as she folded the washing.

"He stinks," added Robby, Kevin's younger brother, after getting a whiff of the sweet-smelling Brylcreem.

"Don't be late home. We gotta fix that fence in the morning," reminded his father as he peered over the top of the newspaper he was reading.

"Everything is ready, I just need to grab the strainer from behind the shed," Kevin replied.

Mr. Hargreaves nodded and returned to the paper and the news stories about the war. "Do you have a lift?" he asked without looking up.

"Ian can't pick me up, his dad's car has a leaky radiator. So I have to walk."

"He should never have bought that car. Norman is such a cheap bastard," Mr. Hargreaves shook his head.

"Francis, please," cautioned Kevin's mum.

"Well, he is cheap." Frank lowered the paper. "You wanna take the truck?"

Kevin's face broke out into a big smile. "Can I?"

"Go ahead, have fun tonight."

Their truck, an old Leyland flatbed, was a bit much for driving to a dance, but it was better than walking. "Thanks, Dad."

The dance was being held at the local community hall. It was organized by the Women's Division of the New Zealand Farmers' Union, known as the WDFU, to raise money for war widows. Kevin and his mates had enthusiastically purchased tickets as it was rumoured the event would attract many single ladies.

With the prospect of meeting the girl of his dreams, Kevin eagerly set off towards the hall, belching an oily cloud of black smoke from the tired Leyland. Finding a park for the large truck proved to be difficult, but in the end, he managed to locate a spot beside a couple of tractors. Careful not to dirty his trousers, he leapt from the cab and checked his hair one final time in the truck's large wing-mirror.

Judging by the strains of music drifting from the hall, the band was already in full swing, and he felt the excitement. He found his comb and slid it smoothly through his hair from front to back a couple of times, pocketed his comb, and adjusted the collar of his shirt before strolling briskly towards the hall, feeling rather debonair and sophisticated.

Suddenly, he didn't feel so confident. As he surveyed the hall and saw all the people dressed in their finest clothes, the beautiful girls looking so fresh and radiant… even the blokes… these were people he knew, his mates, but he hardly recognized them. It was a little overwhelming and now he felt underdressed. This was the first proper dance he'd ever been to, and for the first time in his life, he felt like an adult and wasn't sure he measured up.

With his mouth open, Kevin's head swiveled from side to side as he took in the scene. There were girls everywhere, and they were all dressed to the nines.

"What do ya think, Kev?"

He hadn't seen Ian, his best friend, walk up.

"You said there would be lotsa girls here, but this?"

Ian laughed. "Well, we have the war to thank for that." He gave

Kevin a quick up and down look. "And you're looking dapper."

"Well, thank you, my good man," Kevin said, trying to sound like he was royalty and affecting an upper-crust British accent. "And you are, too."

Ian did a pirouette. "Is my brother's suit. He won't be needing it while he's fighting in the desert. C'mon, let's get a drink."

They threaded their way around groups of people towards a table with a huge glass bowl and helped themselves to a glass of fruit punch.

A group of young men lounged against the wall, clutching their drinks tightly to their chests. Shyly, they watched the girls, many of whom stood against the opposite side of the hall and appraised the young men with equal interest.

A few couples whirled and spun around the dancefloor with ease. Kevin was a little jealous; he wished he was as light on his feet and could master the complexities of dance. He stood amongst the group of young bachelors and watched with envy.

Suddenly, he felt a hand on his shoulder.

"Hiya, Kev. Wanna dance?"

He turned to see Betsy, Ian's younger sister. He didn't have much say in the matter as she took his hand and tugged him towards the dancefloor. "Uh, hi, Bets." He thrust his fruit punch into Ian's hand.

Moments later, she guided him around the floor as his mates watched with glee. Betsy was an attractive young woman, but she was Ian's sister, and therefore off-limits. While Ian enforced the rule of nobody making an improper move on his sibling, that edict was either unknown to Betsy or she simply chose to ignore her older brother's harsh declaration.

Kevin made sure to keep a modest distance from her, lest Ian take offence, and when she steered him close to his mates, he managed to grimace and appear uninterested, purely to demonstrate that he respected and honoured his best friend's wishes. Betsy was a good dancer and gave him some valuable pointers, but he felt awkward and lacked any grace or coordination. After two songs, he managed to spare himself further embarrassment when she had to go to the powder room, and he returned to the glass of fruit punch that Ian held out for him.

"What?" Kevin asked when he saw Ian scowling.

"Don't you go getting ideas, Kev. You'd be the last person I want to see as my brother-in-law."

"Could you imagine us being brothers-in-law?" They both laughed, the incident quickly forgotten.

Kevin continued to peruse the girls on the other side of the hall. He knew most of them, as they were all local. Many had their hair up, and their dresses were so colourful and elegant. They weren't the young gawky girls he went to school with or saw at the shops; these were beautiful and attractive young women. Then, suddenly, he felt guilty. There were more girls here than young men because the men were at war. It didn't seem fair. He looked down at the floor and gave a thought to those brave souls, fighting and giving their lives for freedom while he was here at a dance, surrounded by beautiful ladies. He raised his head and surveyed the hall again, pretty sure that everyone here felt the same. The money raised this evening would go to a worthy cause, and he was only happy to help.

Despite these feelings, his eyes kept returning to look at one young woman, someone he'd never seen before and found her truly captivating.

Kevin turned to Ian, who was explaining the qualities of a good breeding ram to their friend Derek. "Do you know who she is?"

"Who?" Ian turned his head and stared across the room.

"Don't make it obvious. The one on the right in the green and yellow dress."

Ian shook his head. "Don't know her." He turned back to Derek to continue elaborating on the nuances of breeding sheep.

Kevin positioned himself carefully so he could keep an eye on this mystery girl without appearing to ogle.

Chapter Two

Betsy approached. "Kev, let's dance again."

"Thanks, Bets, maybe later."

"No one will dance with me... pleeease?"

Poor Betsy felt the effects of an over-protective brother. Kevin quickly glanced at Ian, but he was still in a deep discussion with Derek.

He looked over Betsy's shoulder at the girl he'd been watching before.

Betsy turned to follow Kevin's gaze. "You fancy her?"

"What? No, no, I was just looking." He felt his cheeks redden.

She giggled. "Oh, you do. I can tell."

"She's alright, I suppose." He shrugged and leaned closer to Betsy so no one could overhear. "Uh, do you know who she is? I was just curious, that's all."

"That's Ruth Downes. Her parents had just bought the Collins' farm on the corner, so she is new here. But I like her, she's very nice... and very pretty." She turned her head to look at him. "And no, she doesn't have a boyfriend."

"Oh, that's good," Kevin replied, happier now that he knew her name and the fact that she was unattached.

One of Betsy's friends, Elizabeth, walked up and the two girls began talking and laughing. Kevin risked another look at Ruth and caught her looking at him in return. He felt his heart begin to pound and his face turn red again. He tried to distract himself and listen to Betsy's conversation with Elizabeth. But it was just *girl talk*, and he quickly lost interest.

He looked over at Ruth and saw her make her way towards the drink table. *Go for it, this is your chance,* he thought. He eased away from Betsy and tried to nonchalantly walk towards the fruit punch to coincide his arrival with hers.

"Please, let me," Kevin offered, extending his hand to Ruth to take her glass and refill it.

She smiled. "Thank you."

He ladled some fruit punch into her glass and tried desperately to think of something to say that wouldn't sound idiotic. He could smell her perfume, and it was intoxicating. He looked up at her. "Uh, the weather's been nice." He quickly turned away and grimaced. *Stupid, stupid, stupid,* he thought.

"We could do with more rain," she answered. Her voice was liquid and mellow.

He swallowed thickly as he tried to think of something intelligent and spark a conversation. Nothing came to mind and he felt awkward; the pause was too long.

"Thank you for the drink." She turned and began to walk away.

"Would you like to dance?" he blurted out.

She turned slowly. It seemed an age before she replied, but it must have been less than a second. "Yes, that would be lovely."

He took her glass and set it next to his on a nearby empty table, then took her hand and led her to the dancefloor as the band began playing a new song.

Before he could position himself, other dancers began gyrating and thrusting out their legs in a wild display of syncopated mayhem. His mouth opened to stare at them while Ruth pulled on his arm to prevent him from being struck by a flailing limb. He awkwardly stepped away and Ruth burst out laughing. "You can jive," she said with a smile; commenting on his quick-step move to avoid being struck.

"What is that?" he asked from the safety of the dancefloor's perimeter. He still held her hand and she hadn't pulled it away.

"I think they call it lundy, or is it the lindy hop? Is an American dance."

"Crikey, it looks dangerous," he said and began to laugh. "Well, whatever it is, I can't dance it. Would you like to sit this one out with me?" He pointed to the table where they left their drinks.

"I can't dance it either," she admitted. "Yes, let's wait until the music is better."

The Women's Division of the New Zealand Farmers' Union had volunteers acting as chaperones, to ensure the young ladies and men behaved appropriately. No alcoholic beverages were being served at this evening's function. Nevertheless, Kevin's friend Derek had produced his father's silver engraved hip flask and claimed he had filled it with some of his mother's finest gin. He'd generously offered his mates a drink in the toilets, but after a few people took hasty gulps, word soon spread that it wasn't gin at all, but rubbing alcohol. Derek denied the allegation emphatically and, to prove his point, upended the flask and drunk a substantial portion. A short time later, he became sick and was taken home by a chaperone.

Both parents were embarrassed and apologized profusely to the chaperone after he drove Derek home.

Punishment was deemed to be time served. Derek had suffered through a very trying ordeal and was lucky not to have caused himself any lasting damage. As Derek's mother explained, the rubbing alcohol was normally stored in the shed, and she had filled an empty gin bottle with it in the event they experienced a medical emergency and needed to use alcohol to clean and disinfect a wound. Derek's father angrily insisted he purchase a replacement flask. Even after numerous washings, the odor and distinct taste remained. Derek quietly admitted that he'd never tasted gin before and believed this was what he'd been drinking.

Kevin and Ruth had been so engrossed with each other that they never heard the commotion when Derek was carried out of the hall, nor were they aware of the time. So it came as some surprise to them when a chaperone approached their table and informed the couple that the evening had come to an end and it was time to go home. Miss Downes' father was outside, waiting for his daughter.

"I, uh, I would like to see you again. Would that be acceptable?" Kevin asked.

She smiled. "You're such a gentleman. But of course."

"Your mum and dad won't mind? I mean, they don't know me or my parents, and I'd hate for you to get in trouble."

"Come, Kevin, you can meet dad now."

The couple said farewell to friends, thanked the chaperones, and walked outside.

"Dad, this is Kevin Hargreaves," said Ruth to her father, who sat in his car outside the hall. "I met him this evening."

"Good evening, sir," said Kevin, hoping to sound intelligent and respectful. It was dark and difficult to see Mr. Downes' face and reaction.

"Did you have a good time?" he asked, giving Kevin a quick look through the open window.

"Oh yes, the band was very good," Ruth replied.

Mr. Downes nodded. "So, do you need a lift home, son?"

"Uh, no, thanks, Mr. Downes. Thanks for asking."

"Alright, then. Hop in, Ruthy, it's late and past my bedtime."

Ruth looked up at Kevin, smiled, walked to the passenger door, and stepped in.

"Good night, Ruth, and nice to meet ya, Mr. Downes."

Mr. Downes grunted and crunched the gears, and the car sputtered away. Kevin felt his heart flutter when he saw Ruth twist in her seat and wave. He stood with his hands in his pockets and watched the dim orange glow of headlights disappear into the night.

Chapter Three

Kevin didn't know much about love. If asked, he would have said he loved his dog and horse, and of course his parents and younger brother too, but when it came to understanding and acknowledging how he felt about Miss Ruth Downes, he was in a quandary. Over the months, he and Ruth spent more and more time together, and his feelings towards her grew. When they first met, he found her to be simply beautiful, witty, and engaging, but now, when he looked at her, she was just flawless. When she looked at him, he felt special, as if he was the only person in the entire world. When she spoke, her words were carefully considered and he listened with rapt attention, often forgetting to reply to a question. The sound of her voice was lilting, soft and melodic, and during the day he'd recall conversations they'd had and how much he enjoyed hearing her speak.

Water gurgled gently over moss covered rocks and disappeared around a bend where the creek would feed into a larger river. Kevin and Ruth lay on a blanket, beneath the shade of a willow tree on the bank of the stream and enjoyed the peace and quietness. Birds twittered high in the branches above them and it was idyllic and, he thought, romantic – he'd brought her here for a reason.

He rolled onto his side and reached for her hand. The softness of her skin was incredible; her touch sent shivers up his spine and he wondered for the umpteenth time if this unusual feeling was the *love* people wrote and spoke of. He couldn't imagine a life without her. "Ruthy?"

"Yes?" she replied, slowly drawing the word out.

He saw her smile. The corners of her mouth twitched ever so slightly. "Uh, I, um…"

She remained silent and stared up at the tree's leafy hanging branches.

"I love you." He winced; this wasn't how he wanted to tell her. He quickly rolled on to his back. "I mean–"

She sat up and leaned over him, her hair spilling onto his face. Her expression silenced him immediately. She looked down on him. Her intense gaze was soft and calming and without reproach. Her eyes sparkled as she squeezed his hand and clutched it tightly to her chest. She lowered her head and they kissed.

Ruth said it was love, and that love was a gift from God to be cherished and treasured forever. He tried to analyze his emotions, but couldn't compare the love he felt for his dog, or his horse, with the new and unfamiliar feelings he had for her. He was sailing in unknown waters, so he simply explained to her how he felt. She didn't laugh or make fun of him; she just smiled and held his hand a little tighter. He breathed in her smell and felt safe. Yes, he'd grown to love her, and she loved him. Of that, there was no doubt.

Ruth Downes was an only child, and both her mother and father doted on her. Frequently, Kevin would visit Ruth and help Mr. Downes with a chore or a job that needed an extra hand. He didn't mind and was happy to do what he could, and Ruth's parents felt comfort in knowing this decent young man was hardworking, respectful, and treated their daughter well. Privately, they admitted he'd make a fine son-in-law and welcomed him into their home and lives as if he was one of the family.

When Ruth was at Kevin's home, she would help his mum around the house, pick fruit from the orchard, and occasionally even cook dinner. Over time, Kevin and Ruth became inseparable. As young couples did, they planned for an uncertain future together that was overshadowed by a brutal war.

Kevin's mum sat at the kitchen table and dabbed at her eyes with a handkerchief, while her husband looked stoically at the far wall. Neither spoke; both were lost in private introspection and shared fears. The newspaper lay open on the table, its printed words more powerful and potent than spoken utterances. The printed text could be read repeatedly, exacting and precise, with no room for misinterpretation or error. The cold, black typeface of the paper's printed words struck savagely at the heart of the Hargreaves family. The words weren't kind, empathetic, or conciliatory, but nor were they unexpected.

The kitchen door flew open and Kevin stuck his head in. "I'm off to see Ruthy..."

He saw his mother's tears fall on the paper. His father's mouth tightened as he slowly turned his head to face his oldest son. "Kev."

Kevin didn't have to read the paper to know. He'd turned nineteen only a month ago and knew the requirements for the military ballot. He stepped into the room and hugged his mother. She twisted in her seat and wrapped both arms tightly around him, and with a groan, buried her head in his shoulder and wept. Mr. Hargreaves turned away, fighting to remain in control. Kevin was of age, and they all knew the day would come when his name was drawn in the ballot.

Kevin and Ruth walked silently out of her house, along a path, through a gate, and into her father's strawberry fields. The young couple ignored the fruit and walked between neatly aligned rows towards a large macrocarpa tree that stood sentinel at the end. Beneath its huge branches, a seat suspended by rope barely moved in the early evening stillness. A blackbird screeched and flew away with indignance at the unwelcome intrusion.

Ruth eased herself onto the seat and melted into Kevin's waiting arms. His chest rose and fell with pent-up anxiousness as he struggled to find the words to tell her.

"I know, Kevin." Her voice sounded sultry and smooth. "Dad showed me the paper. He saw your name came up in the ballot."

He felt her shudder and pulled her in closer. Their heartbeats synchronized and settled into an uncertain rhythm. "We should have talked about it before; I knew this would happen, but I didn't want to accept it." He took a breath. "I'm so sorry, Ruthy."

She was silent for a moment. "We both knew it was inevitable, Kevin, and it isn't your fault. It isn't anyone's fault. How are your mum and dad?"

"Mum's not taking it well, and Dad? You know him. 'We do what we must for king and country'," he mimicked. "And then he gave me his speech about the war and our duty."

"You'll come back, Kev. You'll return home to me. I know this, I feel it. It's just that I will miss you and don't know how long you'll be away."

"I will come back."

"Promise?"

"Yes, I promise."

For Kevin and Ruth, the following days were a blur as Kevin prepared to leave for military training. He was fortunate, as he only had to travel a short distance to camp at Booths Farm in Carterton and hoped he could return home on weekend leave until he deployed. They spent considerable time together, discussing their future and making plans.

Mr. and Mrs. Downes invited the entire Hargreaves family to din-

141

ner at their home. It wasn't the first occasion on which they'd spent time together, but now it was different. The invitation was well-received, as both families had grown close and developed a strong friendship.

It came as no surprise to anyone when Kevin announced during dinner that he had asked Ruth to become his wife and, with a huge grin, added that she'd accepted his proposal. Amidst a jubilant chorus of congratulations, he informed everyone that they would marry when he returned home, but the somber reality of a vicious war and the quickly approaching date of Kevin's departure hung over both families like a dark cloud.

Chapter Four

Bold newspaper headlines wrote of hard-fought victories and oppressing losses, and for the young couple, it was hard to go about their lives without being constantly reminded of death and battles lost in the vastness of Europe, the expanse of Africa, and the Pacific.

"These brave men," began Ruth while they picked fruit in her father's orchard. "They're also sons, brothers, fathers, and husbands…"

Kevin straightened and turned towards her.

"They're more than mere soldiers, yet that's what we call them. But they aren't. Don't you see, Kevin? They're just people with families, like us."

"Ruthy?"

"Listen, please… why must you go and fight in another country? Isn't there a way…?"

He could see she was upset, and he quickly placed his basket onto a cart and took a few steps towards her. She came into his arms and he held her tightly. "Ruthy, unless I'm disabled, ill, or a convict, I have no choice. They tell us we fight for our freedom and to protect the world from an oppressive regime. What should I do when other men, Kiwis, have given their lives to keep us safe? I must do my duty too."

"And I want you to do your part, but I do not want the man I love, my fiancé, to travel to the far side of the world and fight another man's war."

"Then what do you suggest?"

She began to sob, and he stroked her hair and back to comfort her. "Kevin Hargreaves, this is my dilemma. My logical mind tells me that fighting a *just* war is the right thing. But as a young woman, I cannot reconcile myself to the notion that the man I love will leave me for God knows how long, and risk his life fighting on distant shores in another country."

"Then I vow to return and whisk my bride away so we can raise a family and live happily ever after."

She pried herself from his embrace and stepped back to better see his face. "If you do what is asked of you and go to war, then I shall remain strong and wait for you to come back. But come home you must."

Kevin looked into the deep liquid pools of her eyes and saw her pain. *If only there was another way*, he thought. He quickly dismissed the notion and shook his head. "Ruthy, if there was a way for me to avoid going to war and I remained here, how would we both feel when we walked in the street or went shopping, knowing we didn't do our part while others did? That people we don't know gave their lives for us?"

Tears ran freely down Ruth's face, her eyes glistening in understanding and acceptance.

He returned her look, his own eyes moist. "I couldn't live that way, and neither could you."

"This is why I love you, Kevin. We will endure, won't we?"

His mouth tightened. "We have little choice, but we have each other and the strength of our love will see us through."

She stepped towards him and he hugged her tightly.

Mr. Downes watched them from the other side of the hedge as they comforted each other. He understood what the couple was going through. He had fought in the Great War, and by the grace of God, survived physical injury. Yet he still woke at night, drenched with sweat, his mind cruelly recounting the horrors in an endless spectacle of terror-filled memories. Without question, he knew his future son-in-law, if he survived and returned home, would also suffer sleepless nights as he recollected the horrors, like vivid highlights of abomination that would endlessly torment and disturb. The anxiety Ruth presently felt would be replaced by helplessness and inadequacy, for a returned soldier is never the same. Part of him always remains on a battlefield.

A vein pulsed on his neck. He wished he could tell them both to run, flee the call to action, ignore the call to duty, as the cost of going to war on a man's soul, far exceeds his personal sacrifice. He sighed. He couldn't tell them to run and hide – that would be wrong. Although she didn't know it, Ruth would need him; for now, it was his duty to prepare his daughter for the days and nights ahead. He blinked away his tears and turned from them. *May God spare them both.*

The day finally arrived for Kevin to depart for training. He hadn't slept, not because he feared the journey ahead, but because of Ruth. He would miss her, and already he felt the unfamiliar pangs of loss.

Ruth and her parents arrived early at the Hargreaves home. They would have a morning cuppa, say farewell to Kevin, and then return home while Ruth remained and traveled with Kevin's parents to the bus terminal where they would say their goodbyes.

Conversation was stilted and uncomfortable. Kevin's mother kept asking if he'd packed everything he needed, and did he have his paperwork and toothbrush? He repeatedly told her he had, and not to worry. No one wanted to discuss the latest developments of the war in Europe in case it upset Ruth and both mothers, so the conversation centred around farming and agriculture, a safe topic everyone could participate in.

Kevin and Ruth separated themselves from both sets of parents and went for a short walk. Both were aware this would be the last time they'd be alone together in quite some time. Words didn't come easy; there was little to be said that hadn't been previously discussed. All they both wanted was to be close to one another and not have to say goodbye.

It was when they approached the chook-house that Ruth finally broke down. Without restraint, she clung desperately to him and professed her love repeatedly. She showered him with kisses and tears, and cupped his face in her hands as she wept. "I will never let you go," she cried. "While you may have to leave, I will always be with you, at your side." Her chest heaved as she surrendered to his arms.

With a heavy heart, they all arrived at the bus terminal. Saying goodbye was more painful than he imagined, and he struggled to control his emotions as his mother cried. As always, his father showed restraint, yet beneath the shade of his hat, Kevin saw his lip quiver. It wasn't easy for anyone, especially Ruth. Kevin's last sight of her as the bus pulled away was of her mother putting her arms around her and holding her tight. His dad stood alone, resolutely, unmoving, with hands buried deep in his pockets as he stared at the departing bus.

Chapter Five

Training had been difficult for Kevin. Prior to leaving for Booths Farm, Mr. Downes had taken him aside and told him his best chance of staying alive was to embrace and learn all he could about military tactics. "It'll improve your odds, son," he advised.

With diligence, and with Mr. Downes' words still echoing in his head, Kevin applied himself with grit and dogged determination, and performed remarkably well. He wrote to Ruth every day and received her loving letters in return. When the mail was delivered, he was first in line and, with jeers and good-natured ribbing from others, grabbed his bundle of letters and rushed to his bunk to read and savour each cherished word.

The days turned into weeks, and soon they were preparing to deploy. The 2nd New Zealand Expeditionary Force was to divert to Britain, and the day of their sailing was fast approaching. Corporal Kevin Hargreaves had plenty to do, but he still found time to write to his dear Ruthy. His heart ached for her, and he wished, beyond anything else, that he could hold her in his arms, or even see her one last time before he left New Zealand.

The battalion arrived in Wellington and lined up on the docks. The ship's sheer sides towered above them while cranes hoisted equipment and vehicles into the bowels of the ship with tireless energy. The docks were frantic with activity; it was chaotic and, for the departing soldiers, both exhilarating and frightening.

Under the gloom of seeing their loved ones depart, well-wishers were roped off safely to the side where they couldn't impede progress. Officers barked orders and issued commands, and like a serpentine monster, tendrils of men hoisted their kits and wound their way in an endless khaki column around cranes and equipment and onto gangways to disappear into the ship they would call home.

Kevin felt the knot of anxiety tug at his stomach. This was real; he was departing his home and going to war. Automatically, he turned behind and quickly scanned the faces of well-wishers, hoping to glimpse his dear Ruthy. He knew she couldn't come here; it was too far from Wairarapa to Wellington, but he just couldn't help himself and searched for her anyway.

It was now his platoon's turn. With kits hoisted, they shuffled a few steps and slowly began to move towards a gangway. A few policemen stood nearby and ignored the brave men who passed them, choosing to scan the crowd for unruly troublemakers.

The gangway creaked and swayed ever so slightly as it bore the weight of nervous men, most of whom had never been aboard an ocean-going ship before.

"Move along quickly, now!" barked an authoritative voice.

It did little good; soldiers shuffled forward, first one step, then two, and then stopped.

Kevin stepped onto the gangway and paused as a holdup further forward prevented him from advancing. Below him, people waved and shouted tearful farewells. He looked through the hatch and into the ship, and all he saw was a sea of khaki, some sailors, and a pretentious officer with a clipboard. Soon he would board, find a berth, and write another letter. *Hurry up*, he thought, impatient to be underway.

Through the cacophony of brusque military jargon, wharfies yelling at each other, and sorrowful well-wishers endlessly yelling farewell, he heard his name.

In reflex, he turned.

"Kevin!"

He knew that voice. Like a moth drawn to a flame, his eyes settled on her. There was Ruthy. He dropped his kitbag and leapt up and down. "Ruth!" His grin extended from ear to ear and he waved frantically. She saw him and his heart melted. Even from the gangway, he could see her radiant smile. Beside her, there were his mum, dad, and even Robby. He was too far away to hear his mother's choked plea to come home safely, or see the trembling hand of his father. Around them, other families, mothers, fathers, wives, and girlfriends wept for their loved ones; for many, the pain and heartache of loss would never cease. He was moved, knowing they'd driven all this way to see him off.

Ruth called his name again. The sweet liquid sound of her voice cut through the din and instantly calmed him; he heard her so clearly, like magic. Crystal clear. She blew him a kiss, and then he was jostled forward, and with a huge smile still plastered to his face, he was sucked into the ship's belly.

Epilogue

Ruth waved goodbye to Mr. and Mrs. Hargreaves after having lunch with them and walked up the driveway towards her home. She visited Kevin's parents almost daily, and they would each share news from letters that Kevin sent after the mail had been delivered. Her visits were more than welcomed, they were needed, providing a link to their son who they missed so much. For Ruth, the visits brought her closer to Kevin as she listened to endless stories about his childhood that his parents shared so willingly. They all missed him terribly and the growing bond between them blossomed.

It would only take fifteen minutes for Ruth to walk home, and as she did every visit, she declined an offer for a ride. She used the time spent walking to think about Kevin and imagine where he was and what he was doing.

She heard a vehicle approach and looked up. It slowed to a crawl, then turned into the Hargreaves driveway. She stopped and saw the man at the wheel. It was Mr. Simmons, the post-master. He gave her a small wave and continued past, towards the house.

Mr. and Mrs. Hargreaves still stood on the porch and watched as the car came to a stop. Ruth paused and turned to look back behind. She saw Mr. Simmons alight his car, put on his hat and walk towards Kevin's parents.

She felt a chill and folded her arms. Although she was too far away to hear the conversation, she saw them speak briefly and then Mr. Simmons handed a letter to Mr. Hargreaves. Before the letter was opened, Mr. Simmons returned to his car, turned, and moved back up the drive. He didn't wave as he passed her by.

Ruth took an involuntary step closer back towards the house and then stopped when she heard Mrs. Hargreaves cry out. Mr. Hargreaves held the distinctive yellow telegram in his hand as he reached for his wife. Ruth heard her wail and, with a shattered heart, she sank to her knees. Both her hands covered her face as she broke down and wept in grief.

"This is no war of chieftains or of princes, or dynasties or national ambition; it is a war of people and causes. There are vast numbers, not only in this island but in every land, who will render faithful service in this war but whose names will never be known, whose deeds will never be recorded. This is a war of the Unknown Warriors; but let all strive without failing in faith or in duty, and the dark curse of Hitler will be lifted from our age."

Winston Churchill,
Radio Broadcast,
July 14th, 1940

The Mechanic

Chapter One

Central North Island, 1965

Miss Emily Scarborough carefully opened the living room curtains, just enough to have a little peek and remain undetected, and peered through the window and into the night. In the distance, she saw the yellow beams from a pair of vehicle headlights swing across a paddock, then settle on the road as a car safely manoeuvred around a corner and accelerated past her home on the straight. A cloud of dust billowed up and outward, mingling with the sound of the vehicle's throaty exhaust as the car disappeared around the next corner towards town.

"Emily, dear, come away from the window. Your tea is getting cold," advised her older sister, Janine.

Emily closed the curtains and ensured they hung as they should, unruffled, with the creases straight, and returned to her chair and cup of tea. "It's that Harbuck boy, drives like a lunatic," Emily tut-tutted as she sat down and smoothed her dress.

"Pardon?"

"That Harbuck boy… his driving…!" Emily repeated loudly to her sister.

"Oh. He'll have an accident one day," Janine said with a disapproving shake of her head.

"I'm going to call the police. I'm tired of this and they need to do more about these lawbreakers," Emily declared as she unexpectedly rose from her chair.

"Where are you going? Your tea!"

Emily ignored her sister's plea and walked from the living room into the hallway, where the phone sat on a small shelf. She picked up the handset and heard a conversation going on. Without hesitation, she replaced it with a clatter. "That woman is always on the telephone. I swear she has nothing better to do than gossip. Doesn't she realise it's a party-line and other people may need to use the telephone from time to time?" She sighed heavily and returned to her chair. "Sometimes I wonder what the world is coming to." She picked up her cup and took a sip. "My tea is cold."

"What did you say?" asked Janine.

"My tea is cold!"

"Oh. Then go to the police tomorrow, dear," said Janine as she resumed her knitting, the clack of needles competing with the tick-tock of the grandfather clock against the far wall. "Perhaps the constable will have a friendly chat with Mr. Harbuck about his boy."

Emily grunted. "He needs more than a talking to. Mr. Harbuck needs to use his belt and teach that boy some manners and how to drive and behave responsibly." She folded her arms and glared at her cup of tea.

"Then drop by the police station tomorrow," Janine repeated helpfully.

Emily and Janine Scarborough owned and operated the

haberdashery shop in Takipo, a rural community of about ten thousand residents in the central North Island. The two spinsters lived together in a small cottage they owned, about one mile from town. Each morning they'd leave their small home, with Emily driving their light blue Morris Minor, and always arrive at the shop in time, to open at exactly 9:00 am.

Janine would unlock the front door and turn on the lights while Emily collected the cash register drawer from the locked wardrobe in the office. Once the till was ready and they could make a sale, she'd put the kettle on for a morning cuppa as they waited for their first customer.

Emily stood near the cash register and stared reflectively out of the front window of their shop. After a few moments, she turned to Janine, who was creating a colourful, pyramid-shaped display of stacked wool skeins. "I think I will visit the police this morning and have a quiet word with Constable Miller. Is about time he put an end to the shenanigans of that Harbuck boy."

"Pardon?"

"I'm going to the police!"

"Oh, yes, a good idea," said Janine without looking up. "And while you're there, talk to him about that Harbuck boy."

Emily sighed. "Will you be OK by yourself?" she asked in a loud voice.

"Yes, dear, run along. I'll be fine."

Constable Rodney Miller was in the front office, seated behind the reception desk of Takipo's police station and reading the newspaper. He and his wife lived at the rear of the police station, which had been converted from a regular house some years ago. He was enjoying the quietness of another uneventful morning when the little bell above the door jingled. He looked up in some surprise at the unexpected caller. "Good morning, Miss Scarborough." He neatly folded the paper, placed it aside on his desk, and stood as he greeted her.

Emily looked apprehensive. "Good morning, Constable," she replied tightly clutching her handbag.

"I, uh, don't believe I've had the pleasure of seeing you here before. How can I assist you? Is everything OK?" he inquired and leaned forward with both arms resting on the counter, eager to learn the reason for her visit.

"Is that Harbuck boy. Driving like a madman, he is. He zooms past our house at all sorts of times, making a horrible noise, creating dust and driving way too fast." She frowned to emphasise her point. "One day he'll kill someone, or himself."

"I see… Uh, that would be Colin Harbuck," the constable informed. "I've had cause to issue him with an infringement notice on more than one occasion, he–"

"You need to speak with his father, have him take to the boy. He needs a good strapping," she interrupted.

"When did the incident occur?"

"Last night, at nine-thirty to be precise."

"Rest assured, Miss Scarborough, I'll pay young Mr. Harbuck a visit and put an end to it, eh?"

"I certainly hope so. Isn't like you are overworked or anything," she said rather coldly and turned to glance at some pamphlets and brochures stacked on the side of the counter. "Very well, I'll be on my way. Good day."

Constable Rodney Miller watched her as she walked towards the door. "Have a lovely day."

Emily twisted her head and gave a forced smile before leaving.

He sighed loudly as the door closed. "So that little shit Colin Harbuck is at it again, is he? I'll get the bugger," he said to himself, then looked at the clock on the wall. It was time for his morning patrol and he was going to pay Colin Harbuck a friendly visit.

Chapter Two

Constable Rodney Miller was proud of his police car. It was a shiny, black EH Holden with a powerful six-cylinder motor. When needed, the car could put on a surprising turn of speed, and it handled remarkably well. On its roof was a red cherry, and to Rodney, it was more than an emergency light. It was a symbol of his authority, "...a beacon of righteousness," he told his wife on more than one occasion. He eyed the car carefully, looking for flecks of dirt as he fished for his keys. With the car unlocked, he threw his hat on the passenger seat, placed the key in the ignition, and started the motor. He loved his patrol car.

He knew where Colin Harbuck worked. He was an apprentice motor mechanic at Takipo Motors, and Rodney was very familiar with the establishment. It happened to be the same garage that serviced his police car. With a little tyre chirp, the policeman exited his driveway and headed for Queen Street.

He didn't need to drive far. He cruised down Takipo's main street, occasionally waving to someone he recognised, and diligently scanning the footpath and road ahead, always on the lookout for miscreants or speeders. The police radio squelched every now and then, but there wasn't much of interest to be heard, so he turned the volume down a little.

As he turned the corner onto Queen Street, he saw a Cortina approach. Without warning, the driver slammed on the brakes. The car skidded briefly, then continued slowly towards the workshop of Takipo Motors. Constable Miller flicked on his indicator and turned into the garage to follow just as young Colin Harbuck stepped from the white Cortina.

Constable Miller quickly parked, reached for his hat, exited his Holden, and adjusted his black blazer as he met the eye of the young apprentice. "What was the hurry, Colin?"

"Hello, Officer," Colin politely greeted the policeman. He looked puzzled. "Hurry?"

Constable Miller raised an arm and pointed towards the road, where only moments before, he'd witnessed the Cortina with its tyres locked up, sliding along.

"Oh, that," Colin replied with a smile. "I just fixed the brakes on this," he patted the fender of the Cortina, "and I needed to test them. We always test the brakes on customers' cars just outside the garage on the street. Is the safest place to do it."

Constable Miller chewed his lip. "I'm a little concerned about your driving habits, young man. Seems there have been a number of complaints made against you."

"What complaints? What are you talking about?" Colin looked puzzled and shook his head in denial.

"I think you are well aware of your penchant for driving recklessly. You constantly exceed the posted speed limit and drive way too fast." Rodney leaned forward. "It's going to stop, do you understand me?"

Colin scratched his unruly mop of blonde hair. "You've ticketed me twice. Both times I was going just over the thirty mile per hour speed limit. I don't drive dangerously. Who reported me and where was I speeding?"

Miller smiled. "I have it on good authority that you use Wakefield Creek Road as your personal race-track. But no more." Constable Miller raised his hand and pointed a finger at Colin's chest. "Got it?"

Colin was frustrated. "Constable, Wakefield Creek Road is posted as 'Open Road'. It isn't possible to drive at the maximum speed limit there. It's a gravel road, narrow, and winding so how can I speed on it?"

"Reckless driving," frowned Constable Miller and flicked his ticket book open.

"Are you giving me a ticket?" Colin asked incredulously, his eyes open wide in astonishment.

"Let me see your license," the constable demanded, ignoring the question. He extended a hand and curled his fingers repeatedly. "License."

Colin reached into his overalls, extracted the small, dark-cover booklet from his wallet, and reluctantly handed it over.

Miller copied the particulars and proceeded to complete the infringement details.

"What's the ticket for?"

"Reckless driving," stated the policeman with the assuredness of his authority.

"Where?

"Right here on Queen Street." Miller looked at his wristwatch and logged the time.

"I can't believe you're doing this. We always test the brakes outside the garage and have done so for years. Where can we do it if you won't allow us to do that here anymore?" Colin looked to see if his boss had returned from picking up parts. He'd want to learn of this.

"That is your problem, not mine." Rodney returned Colin's license, and then, with a dramatic flourish, tore a copy of the infringement notice from his book and handed it to Colin. "My suggestion to you – drive responsibly, drive within the posted speed limits, and you won't have any trouble from me." Constable Miller smiled at the young man and walked back to the patrol car with a slight swagger.

Colin stood staring, one hand buried in his overalls' pocket and the other clutching a crumpled ticket. "Bastard," he said quietly.

Miller paused and turned his head. "What was that you said?"

Colin shook his head. "I didn't say anything."

The next day, Colin recounted his altercation with Constable Miller to his mum and dad as they sat at the kitchen table, eating breakfast. He still lived at home with his parents, and had an older sister who was at Teachers' Training College in Wellington. His father, Ian, was a traveling fertilizer salesman, and his mum, Diane, worked part-time at the Clarendon pub as a cook.

"To be honest, Constable Miller has a point," Ian stated as he chewed on a slice of toast. "Why should the law be any different for you just because you're repairing a car?"

"Where does it say that testing the brakes is reckless driving? It isn't. That constable just doesn't like me, he's always picking on me. Now I have another ticket to pay, and it isn't like I'm earning good money or anything," said Colin, looking at his father's breakfast plate. "How come you're not having eggs this morning?"

"He still has const– uh, he is a little, uh, bound up," said Diane with a coy smile.

Colin laughed.

"Don't laugh," said his father, trying to keep a straight face. "Happens to us all at some time or other."

"I gave him a laxative. That should solve the problem," Diane said as she gave her husband an affectionate pat on his shoulder. "But we really shouldn't discuss this at the table."

Colin grimaced.

"Colin, you need to drive in such a way that you don't attract attention or get more tickets," Diane said as she began clearing the table.

"Your Mum's right, Colin. Don't speed and don't give the constable an excuse to go after you," his dad added. "I have yet to get a ticket in all the years I've been driving, and I don't know how you always seem to get them."

Colin rose from his seat and laughed. "That's because that Austin piece of junk you drive can't go past the speed limit. I gotta go to work."

The Ford Consul had seen better days. It suffered from rust and had some engine problems, but Colin had purchased the car cheaply and vowed to restore it to its former glory. He'd fixed the mechanical problems, noticeably improved performance, and was still working on various parts of the body. The exhaust system wasn't standard, and it was considerably louder than normal. Nonetheless, Colin was proud of his car and all the work he had done on it so far.

After saying goodbye to his parents, he climbed in his car and drove sedately down Wakefield Creek Road towards town. On the way, he thought about the unfairness of the ticket he'd received. Dust billowed behind him as he navigated sharp corners with gravel banked high on the sides. He avoided deep, jarring potholes and crossed over a one-lane bridge. It came as a surprise when he encountered the light blue Morris Minor that belonged to the Scarborough sisters sitting in the middle of the road.

He eased to a stop behind the Morris and stepped from his car as Emily Scarborough climbed from her vehicle, waving a handkerchief to ward off the dust that settled over everything.

"Thank goodness you were passing," said Emily, looking distraught and still waving her handkerchief.

"What happened? Are you OK?" Colin asked, looking closely for damage or sign of an accident. He saw the other Miss Scarborough was still in the Morris's passenger seat.

"We were driving to town, and all of a sudden, the engine stopped for no reason at all," Emily said. "I think the motor has had it. We've been sitting here stranded, waiting for someone to help us," she informed Colin. "We're very late opening the shop."

"May I have a look? Perhaps I can help," he kindly offered.

"Or you can drive us to town," she simply stated.

"If you can, open the bonnet. Try to start the motor, but only when I tell you," Colin instructed. He moved to the front as Emily climbed back inside and released the bonnet catch. A moment later, the starter motor began turning, and Colin jerked his hand back from the engine bay. He hadn't told her to start the motor. Had he been less lucky, he could have seriously injured his hand.

"Stop!" he yelled.

He should have heard a clicking sound coming from beneath the bonnet. It was quiet.

"Hang on a sec! Don't do anything!" Colin reached for a fist-sized rock from the side of the road and gently hit the petrol pump with it twice. "Alright, try now!" he yelled after making sure his hands were safely away from the motor.

Emily turned the key and immediately he heard the familiar clicking sound as she cranked the motor again, and within seconds, the engine fired and purred into life. Colin lowered the bonnet and stepped around the car to explain what was wrong, when the Morris suddenly lurched forward and shot off. Emily waved once and left him in a small cloud of dust.

Chapter Three

Constable Miller was peeved. He'd spent the best part of his breakfast time explaining to his wife how the youth of today showed no respect for the laws of the land or their elders, and deliberately flouted authority at every opportunity. As an example, he cited eighteen-year-old Colin Harbuck. "The young man needs to respect authority," he told her.

Rodney's wife listened attentively, nodded supportively at the appropriate times, and commiserated at the state of today's young people's abhorrent and selfish attitudes. Not blessed with having any children of their own, Mr. and Mrs. Miller felt it their duty to right social injustices, especially Rodney in his capacity of Takipo's resident constable. "The only way that Harbuck lad will make something of himself is if he joins the army and learns some discipline, and that isn't likely to happen any time soon, is it?"

"No, dear, it isn't," Mrs. Miller replied.

"The best thing I can do is keep an eye on him... for his own good, mind you, and let him learn to accept the consequences of misbehaviour and law-breaking. Is the only way he will learn."

At five o'clock, Constable Miller was seated in his patrol car near the intersection of Main Road and Wakefield Creek Road. He'd parked in such a way that he could clearly see if any drivers ignored the 'Stop' sign.

Just as he anticipated, the cream Ford Consul with a red mud guard and loud exhaust arrived and slowed down to stop. Colin Harbuck was on his way home from work, he observed. Constable Miller squinted and watched through the windscreen carefully. *Did the vehicle come to a complete stop?* From his angle, it appeared the wheels hadn't quite stopped rotating– there was some movement. The Ford Consul picked up speed, accelerated through the intersection, and continued down Wakefield Creek Road slightly below the speed limit.

Constable Miller grinned and flicked a switch on his dashboard. The emergency cherry light on the roof blazed red, and with another click, the siren began to wail. He muted the siren when he saw the Consul's brake-lights flash and then remain on as the car pulled over to the side of the road.

He took his time, slowly stepped from his patrol car, put his hat on, and, with his ticket book in hand, strode confidently to the Ford Consul. "Good afternoon. May I see your driver's license, please?"

"What did I do?" Colin questioned through the window.

"Failure to come to a complete stop at a controlled intersection when directed to do so by a clearly marked sign. License, please."

Colin handed his license over as instructed. "I did stop. I came to a complete stop, you can't give me a ticket," he appealed.

Constable Miller leaned down so he could see Colin's face clearly. "When will you learn, eh? I'm ticketing you for failing to stop. Consider yourself bloody lucky I didn't find something else to ticket you for. I'm sure that if I looked, there'd be plenty wrong with this vehicle." He straightened.

"I stopped, I came to a stop! Why are you doing this?" Colin seethed.

"If you wish to appeal this infringement notice, you can do so by mail. The address is on the back." Constable Miller tapped the ticket book with his biro and continued writing the ticket.

"Is your word against mine, and who would believe me? You're just picking on me. You know I stopped back there!" he protested loudly.

"If you continue to be unruly, I shall ask you to accompany me to the station," Constable Miller raised his eyebrows, secretly hoping the young man would require restraining.

In frustration, Colin slammed both hands on the steering wheel and shook his head. Wisely, he said nothing more as his latest ticket was handed to him.

"Have a pleasant evening, sir," said the constable with a smirk.

Colin watched him walk back to his car, climb inside, do a U-turn, and drive away, tyres spinning. "Bastard!"

The drive home was a blur as Colin's rage went unchecked. When he told his mother what had happened she yelled at him: "Tell me why a policeman would give you a ticket if you'd done nothing wrong? Why, Colin?"

He shrugged. "Because he doesn't like me, why else?"

"Well, he must have thought you hadn't stopped. Is all I can say on the matter."

"I did stop. Briefly, I admit, but I did come to a complete stop," Colin added.

"And now all your hard-earned wages are going to pay fines." She looked at him with a measure of sympathy and her expression softened. "I tell you what. I need help on Sunday. Maria is having the day off and your dad can't help me, his stomach is still upsetting him."

Colin needed no urging. The money he would earn at the Clarendon for helping his mum cook the Sunday roast dinner was better than his measly hourly wage at the garage. He certainly needed some extra cash. "OK, I'd be happy to help. What's this week's dessert?"

She reached out and gave him a hug. "This week it's vanilla ice-cream and hot chocolate sauce with a sprinkling of hundreds and thousands."

Colin wandered outside to do some sanding on his rusty mud-guard, thinking about the much needed extra money he'd earn on Sunday afternoon.

Helping his mum wasn't hard work. Beginning at lunch time, he would just plate the roast dinner and serve it to the customers when they were ready, including dessert if it was ordered. He liked helping out, and it made a nice change from the garage. He paused in his sanding. "Shit," he muttered. He remembered now, Constable Miller and his wife always came to the Clarendon for Sunday's roast special and dessert; the constable would be there. *Maybe I'll dish him up some bad spuds*, he considered. But then another thought came to mind – revenge. He dropped the sandpaper and stared up at a cloudless sky as a smile creased his face. He turned and ran into the house, heading for the bathroom.

He opened the medicine cabinet and there it was. The turquoise-coloured box stared innocently back at him. Colin grinned and pulled the packet from the shelf to read the instructions at the back.

Adults and children 12 years of age and older, chew 2 chocolated pieces once or twice daily.

He turned the box over and read the writing on the front:

Chocolax, regular strength, family size... real chocolate, gentle acting.

Carefully, he replaced the box, closed the medicine cabinet, and returned outside to his car. He couldn't help laughing. *Wait until Constable 'bloody' Miller eats dessert. Within six hours he'll be in a whole mess of trouble*, he thought. The laxative would kick in, and as he knew, Miller always began his Sunday evening patrol around 6:00 p.m. before returning about 8:00 p.m. The timing was perfect; by then, Colin knew that he'd be finished at the Clarendon, and he'd make sure he was near the police station to see the results of his handiwork. There was no way he'd get caught. Nothing could be proven as long as no one saw him melt the laxative before pouring it over the policeman's ice-cream.

Chapter Four

Saturday was no different than any other day during the week, except Colin only worked half a day. He drove from home and headed down Wakefield Creek Road, and as he approached the Scarborough sisters' house, he saw their Morris Minor halfway across the road just outside their driveway. He gently pulled to the side and parked on the grass verge.

He walked to the car and saw no one. He knew what the Morris's problem was, so he walked up the short driveway and knocked on the door. Within moments, it opened.

"Oh, it's you. I thought it was the tow-truck," said Emily as she looked past Colin and down the road.

"Mornin'. I saw your car, and I know what's wrong with it. I'm sure I can start it and move it for you if you'd like."

"You do?"

"It's the petrol pump. They're electric and always cause problems. I can show you what to do if it doesn't start so you won't be stranded in the middle of nowhere, but you do need to have the pump looked at or replaced."

"I've called a tow-truck. It should be here any moment," she sighed loudly. "Alright, then, show me," Emily said. She turned her head and spoke to her sister inside the house, "I'll be back in a moment, just going to the car."

"What?"

"Back in a tic!" she shouted.

Colin showed her exactly what to do, and sure enough, the car started quickly. He turned the engine off, and then they both heard the sound of gears grinding as a tow-truck appeared, trailing a cloud of dust.

Emily was pleased. "Thank you so much, young man. Now I need to explain to the tow-truck driver he isn't needed."

The truck screeched to a stop and blocked the road. Following behind, Colin saw the distinctive shape of a black police patrol car materialise from the dust and felt his stomach tighten. "I'll wait in my car until the truck moves."

Colin didn't want to engage with the constable and risk further trouble. He climbed in his car as Miller pulled in behind the truck.

"Everything alright, Miss Scarborough?" asked Constable Miller after having a quick word with the tow truck driver. "I had a report that a tow truck was needed up here, and thought I'd make sure there weren't any problems." He looked over at Colin, who was seated quietly in his car, and scowled.

"The car is fine. It stalled and I couldn't start it, but the Harbuck boy kindly fixed it for me and showed me what was wrong. All is well, thank you, Constable."

Miller nodded slowly, turned slightly so that Colin couldn't hear their conversation, and lowered his voice. "After we spoke earlier this week, I had occasion to issue a couple of tickets to him," Miller inclined his head slightly in the direction of Colin. "I doubt he'll be causing you any more problems, Miss Scarborough. He'll be too busy working to pay the fines."

"Oh, dear me. And he's been so helpful, too," she said.

Constable Miller turned to the tow truck to tell the driver he wasn't needed and was free to go. With a gear crunch, the truck managed to turn and eventually drove away after running over one of Emily's roses.

"Thank you, Constable, you may leave now. Janine and I have things to do."

Colin lagged well behind the patrol car as he followed the constable into town. He was relieved Constable Miller didn't speak to him, but he saw the scowls. More than ever, he was determined he would exact revenge.

Helping his mum at the Clarendon wasn't that difficult. He plated every meal just as each customer wanted. Some wanted less peas or more spuds, while others insisted he not be stingy with the gravy or meat. It was the same with their dessert and how much chocolate sauce or hundreds and thousands they wanted.

He felt the nerve jitters when Constable Miller and his wife arrived. His mother took their order and was polite and courteous to them. If the policeman saw him, Colin wasn't aware of it, as he kept his back turned.

Colin looked at the Millers' order and was relieved to see that both of them ordered dessert. He smiled, slipped a hand into his pocket, and felt the Chocolax pieces inside. While his mother was busy slicing meat, he quickly unwrapped the laxative chocolate and placed six pieces in an empty cup, then put the cup in a bowl of boiling water from the kettle. It would take a while to soften, so he continued plating and serving in the meantime.

When it was time to serve the Millers, he felt the anxiety return. He walked to their table, put a plate in front of each of them, and quickly walked away. Mrs. Miller said thank you, while Rodney Miller continued talking to his wife. Colin wasn't sure that the constable even recognised him.

Once back in the kitchen, he checked on the Chocolax. It had melted! Colin smiled.

When customers finished their dinner, they would place their empty plate on a trolley and return to the kitchen counter with their receipt to get dessert. Colin kept an eye on the Millers. After a while, he saw the constable rise from his chair with two empty dinner plates and stack them on the dirty dishes trolley. He walked to the counter and held out his receipt for dessert. "Here's your, uh – ticket." His voice was unnecessarily loud.

Colin felt his face flush red. *The bastard!* He forced himself to be nice and took the receipt. "I'll bring them right over, Mr. Miller."

Constable Miller looked like he was going to say something more, then changed his mind, sneered, and returned to his table.

Colin was furious. *He said 'ticket' to deliberately antagonise me,* he thought as he began to prepare their dessert.

He scooped ice-cream into both bowls, sticking to the correct portion size his mother had shown him, and poured hot chocolate sauce over the icecream in the first dish. Then he carefully checked to make sure no one was looking and poured half the contents of the melted Chocolax over the second bowl. He paused and remembered being issued each of the tickets by Constable Miller, and especially the last humiliating snide comment he made. In a moment of renewed anger, he upended the cup and poured the remaining contents over the ice-cream in the second bowl. A generous portion of hundreds and thousands followed.

He picked up both dishes, walked to the Millers' table, and placed the Chocolax dessert in front of the constable, and the other, untainted bowl in front of his wife. "Enjoy your dessert," he said with a cheery smile.

Constable Miller grunted.

Mrs. Miller said thank you.

As Colin returned to the kitchen he wondered if he'd gone too far. His dad had only taken two pieces of Chocolax, and according to his mum, the stuff had worked a treat. However, he'd just given the constable the equivalent of six pieces of Chocolax – twice the recommended dosage! He stopped and turned to look back at the Millers' table. *Perhaps it's not too late to take it back,* he thought in a brief moment of guilt. The constable was already digging in and wolfing down his ice-cream. It *was* too late. Colin shrugged and looked at the clock on the kitchen wall as he returned to work. He did a quick calculation. "Quarter to seven," he said.

"What did you say?" his mum asked.

"Nothing, I was just thinking." He grinned and began humming a new Beatles song.

Epilogue

Colin sat directly opposite the police station on a bench-seat in Takipo's Veteran's Park. It was a small garden area dedicated to fallen soldiers who'd given their lives in both the first and second world wars. Behind him, a bronze statue of a soldier with a shouldered weapon stared in the same direction. Colin thought it was fitting that both of them had fought for justice. While their causes were remarkably different, he reasoned, philosophically, their goals were similar – to rid the world of oppression and tyranny.

He looked at his wristwatch again. Only five minutes had passed since the last time he looked, and still there was no sign of Constable Miller. He was growing anxious. Perhaps the Chocolax didn't work after it was heated, or maybe the digestive tract of a policeman was considerably different than that of a normal human. He looked down Main Street, first to the right, and then to the left. Nothing – no sign of a police car.

He decided to go home and was about to stand when he heard the sound of a racing engine. He turned to look down the street and saw the black Holden police car power through an intersection without stopping. The back-end of the car swung around as it temporarily lost traction. The driver over-corrected the steering, and the car then swerved in the other direction, wobbled, straightened, and then tore down Main Street towards him. Without slowing, the car veered from the road, ran over a flower bed, shot up the Millers' driveway, and skidded the last twenty feet to a stop.

Colin's mouth hung open. He didn't know whether to laugh or quickly buy an airplane ticket to India and hide for the rest of his life.

The driver's door flew open and Constable Miller staggered out. He bent over with both hands behind, clutching his backside, and ran with an awkward gait towards his residence at the rear of the station. The last thing Colin heard was "Ooooooooooooh!"

He laughed all the way home.

Monday was another typical day for Colin. He didn't see Constable Miller or hear anything about a police car driving dangerously through Takipo the previous evening.

He returned home just in time for dinner and was seated at the table with his father when his mother began serving Clarendon's roast dinner left-overs. "I had a visitor today, Colin," she said.

Colin's eyes opened wide. "Oh?" He looked down at his plate.

"Miss Emily Scarborough and her sister came looking for you."

Colin felt immediate relief and began breathing again. He looked up. "Why would they come here? Were they complaining about my driving?"

"No, on the contrary, they came to offer their thanks for helping them with their car."

"That's nice," Colin replied.

"Yes, it is, and it was lovely of you to help them. They also asked about a ticket you may have received and how much the fine was."

Colin's eyebrows furrowed. "Why would they want to know that?" he asked.

Colin's dad looked on and said nothing.

"Because they wanted to give you a gift." She pulled a five-pound note from her apron and held it up.

"What?" Colin exclaimed.

"Five pounds!" she said. "It's to pay for your ticket."

Colin was speechless for a moment and shook his head in disbelief. "What a nice gesture. I can't believe it."

"Put it in the bank and use it to pay for your tickets," his dad said.

"I will. I promise."

"Colin?" His father spoke again. "Did you hear what happened to Constable Miller last night?"

The pleasurable thought of having money to pay for one of his tickets disappeared in a flash, only to be replaced by an unpleasant feeling of distress. "Uh, no. What happened?" He couldn't meet the eyes of his father and guiltily looked down at his dinner.

"You know who Mac is?"

"Yes, old man MacGregor who drives the beetle," Colin replied.

"At about seven o'clock last night, he was given a speeding ticket by Constable Miller. Seems he was driving thirty-three miles per hour, three miles per hour over the speed limit, when suddenly…" Ian began to laugh. "When suddenly…" He cleared his throat and continued with some effort. "Miller shit himself. Apparently, it ran down the inside of his trousers and onto the street."

Colin's mother began to cough and turned away to hide her face.

"According to Mac, Miller took off, leapt in his patrol car and sped away. No longer able to hold back," Ian burst out laughing.

Colin joined in. This was what he had hoped to hear. *Revenge is sweet.*

With her coughing fit under control, Colin's mum approached and leaned forward over the table. "But what we want to know is, did you have anything to do with it?"

Colin stopped laughing and, as if he saw something fascinating on his plate, stared at it with remarkable concentration. Without looking up, he replied, "Uh, why would you ask?"

"Well, we have a couple of reasons," his mum continued. "Do you know what happened to the Chocolax that was in the medicine cupboard?"

"Er, uh…"

"And when I finished cleaning the kitchen at the Clarendon last night, I saw a cup with the remains of melted chocolate inside. I can't for the life of me figure out why that cup with chocolate sauce would be there. What do you have to say?"

Colin took a deep breath and looked up at his mum to admit his wrongdoing. Her face was bright red, and she was visibly struggling to remain composed – and then she failed.

ASTARDS

Chapter One

Oamaru, 1963

The elderly lady paused briefly outside the entrance to the post office to confirm that her purse and savings passbook were in her handbag. She was a little forgetful these days and constantly needed to double-check to ensure she hadn't forgotten anything when she left her home. She rummaged in her bag, saw the familiar brown purse with the silver clasp and the worn booklet with curled corners and, reassured, stepped from the footpath to enter the building.

There was no line, and she shuffled slowly to the counter, presented her savings passbook, along with a withdrawal slip, to the teller, and smiled. The teller, a friendly woman, made some casual small talk and processed the transaction efficiently, concluding by stamping and then returning the passbook. She reached into the cash drawer, pulled out some crisp and new currency notes, and counted out twenty pounds in various denominations, just as the nice old lady preferred. As protocol demanded, she recounted the money and handed the small bundle over. "Thank you, Mrs. Brewer," she smiled again before looking at the next person who stepped up to wait in line.

Mrs. Eileen Brewer considerately moved aside to make room for the next customer and, with arthritic fingers, fumbled for her purse and placed the money inside, neatly and carefully. Satisfied, she stepped out onto the footpath and collided with a man at the same moment.

She heard a heavy object smash onto the concrete footpath as she stumbled and nearly fell. Thankfully, the quick reaction of the man saved her as he caught her by the arm.

"Oh my!" she gasped, then looked at the ground to see what had broken. She saw a few shards and pieces of broken glass that spilled from a brown paper bag. "Please, forgive me, I... I never saw you," she exclaimed, feeling flustered. She brought her hand to her chest as her heartbeat quickened. She felt quite faint.

"You nearly fell. It was lucky I caught you," said the man, repositioning his hat, which had come askew. "Are you alright? Do you need to sit?" he asked with some concern.

"Thank you, I... think I'm fine," she said. "But your... um, your–"

"Vase. A gift for my mother," He grimaced. Assured the old lady wouldn't keel over, he bent down to pick up the glass pieces and quickly put them back inside the paper bag.

A few people walked around them, as they stood blocking the footpath just outside the post office entrance. After picking up the paper bag, the man gently steered her to the side where they wouldn't be in the way of other pedestrians.

"But your vase... was it expensive?"

He held the paper bag with care to ensure he didn't cut himself on any pieces of broken glass that could poke through. "Yes, it was a bit," he said despondently, "but never mind, as long as you aren't hurt."

The old lady looked thoughtful. "Please, let me pay for it. Perhaps you can purchase another?" She smiled.

"Thank you, you are most kind, but that isn't necessary."

She raised her handbag and searched inside for her brown leather purse. "No, I insist. How much was it?" She looked up at him.

"It cost me five pounds; it was crystal. But you needn't–"

"Oh, it was pricey, wasn't it?" She paused a moment and did some quick calculations. She knew that if she gave the man five pounds, she wouldn't be able to afford having her hair done today. The remaining money was allocated to pay bills. She looked down at the bag with the broken glass in the man's hands and came to a decision. "Please, allow me." She opened her purse, found what she sought and, with a trembling hand, awkwardly extracted a crisp five-pound note. Then she quickly returned the purse to her handbag. "Here," she handed him the money. "I hope you can find another. But I must apologize; I'm so sorry. I... I just didn't see you."

"Thank you very much," he said. "But, er, I really must go. I'm running late."

"Cheerio," said Mrs. Brewer, still feeling a little lightheaded as he quickly strode off. "I should cancel my appointment," she mumbled and slowly headed to the salon two doors down, disappointed she wouldn't have her hair done for the birthday dinner.

Eddie Ricketts walked around the corner and stopped to empty the broken glass from the paper bag into a rubbish bin. He shook the bag a couple of times to remove any fine slivers that were still caught inside, folded it, placed the bag in the pocket of his jacket, and casually wandered away, whistling.

The nearest pub wasn't far, and Eddie sauntered in, purchased a handle of draught beer, and handed a crisp five-pound note to the barman. While waiting for his change, he scanned the room. His dark eyes flicked from person to person and then settled on a suitable place to stand and drink. He thanked the barman with a nod, pocketed his change and ambled through the bar, picking up tidbits of conversation as he wove around thirsty patrons towards the table he selected. With his back to the wall, he leaned against the table, raised the handle to his lips, and took a generous swallow before wiping froth from his mouth.

To anyone watching, he looked like a laid-back, easygoing fellow, but he was far from relaxed. He was on high alert and very attentive. Eddie knew how to fool people; in fact, it was something he was quite proficient at. With surprising skill, he unobtrusively listened to various conversations, picking up little bits of information here and there and discovering quite a bit about the people around him.

One man, a butcher, Eddie learned, was taking orders for meat. It seemed the meat was not legal, and the steer had been stolen, rustled from a local farm. The butcher was cutting the carcass in his shed at home and selling cheap meat to his customers at the pub. Eddie saw opportunity. Just as he was about to go over and have a chat with the man, the butcher drained his glass, told his mates that he'd be back later, and left.

Eddie decided he would also return later. He tilted his head back, emptied the last of his beer into his mouth and, with a tissue, carefully wiped the inside of the dimpled glass mug. After making sure that no one was watching, he extracted the folded paper bag from his pocket, placed the bulky glass mug inside and, after another quick perusal of the room, grabbed an empty handle from a vacant neighboring table and left it on his. He exited the pub after giving the barman a friendly wave.

Just down the road was a bank he'd seen earlier, and he casually strolled towards it with the paper bag containing the glass mug tucked under his arm. His dark eyes flicked from one person to another as he sought his next victim. He knew what he wanted; the elderly were best. It wasn't that old people were easy pickings. They weren't; youngsters were naïve and gullible, but older people had more money, and that was what he wanted.

Eddie Ricketts wasn't a particularly friendly chap. He was a loner and a man of few words, and even fewer sincere words. But when 'on the job', he could be kind, sympathetic, and even charming. As a skilled 'confidence' man, he could gain the trust of someone and take their money, and they wouldn't even know it.

Various police reports stated that he was of average build, five foot ten, with black hair and no distinguishing features. Victims described him as unassuming, with a disarming, pleasant smile. His dark eyes, however, were cold, unfeeling, and vacant. Like any trickster, he was aware of his shortcomings and constantly wore a hat; its shadow beneath a wide brim hid his soulless eyes from the curious.

Eddie pulled a tobacco pouch from his pocket, rolled a cigarette, and watched people from across the street, heading towards the bank. He missed nothing; his eyes, constantly moving, saw every detail. He ignored the young couple and the woman pushing a pram. The businessman wearing an expensive suit and carrying a briefcase held no interest for him. However, his attention was piqued when he saw an elderly man with a walking stick slowly making his way towards the bank's entrance. With the paper bag containing the glass 'handle' from the pub held securely under his arm, he strolled across the road and positioned himself so he could glimpse around the bank's frosted window and determine if the old man was withdrawing money. Most of the time they were; the elderly seldom deposited.

After a minute or two, the old gentleman concluded his business and slowly began to move towards the exit. Eddie flicked his cigarette into the gutter, took a breath, and timed his collision perfectly. The paper bag fell from beneath his arm and crashed onto the footpath.

"Oh, goodness gracious," exclaimed the old man, "I never saw you."

Chapter Two

The banks had all closed, and Eddie Ricketts was again in the pub after a very productive day. By his calculations, he'd made half a week's wages by targeting the elderly today, but couldn't do so anymore, or someone might become suspicious and dob him in. However, there were other opportunities to pursue. He looked over at a neighboring table and observed the butcher, who had returned. From what he garnered, the man had sold a considerable amount of meat and pocketed a sizeable sum of money.

He would wait until the butcher left the pub and then have a chat with him outside, away from eavesdroppers. Eddie sipped his beer and patiently bid his time.

Finally, the butcher called it a night and departed from the pub; Eddie followed half a dozen steps behind.

"You've got a good business going there," said Eddie once they were outside.

The butcher turned and appraised the stranger. "Who wants to know?"

Eddie took a step closer. "Seems to me that you've got plenty of customers but are running low on product." He fished in his pocket for tobacco and began rolling. It wasn't that he needed a smoke; he didn't. It was intended to put the nervous butcher at ease and show the man he wasn't a threat.

"You're a bit of a nosey bugger, aren't ya?" replied the butcher, looking suspicious. "Perhaps you should mind your own business, eh?"

"I'm a businessman, always on the lookout to make a few extra bob or two. Figured we could help each other, especially if you need more, uh, product."

The butcher seemed curious and took a step closer. Eddie knew he had him hooked. Now to reel him in.

"I could always do with more," said the butcher. "But how come you think I don't have enough to supply my customers? Do you know something I don't?"

Now it was Eddie's turn to give the man a good look. He was small, diminutive, and as Eddie knew, small men tended to be cocky to make up for their size. The butcher faced Eddie with his fists clenched aggressively and his arms down the sides of his body as he waited for an answer.

Eddie licked the paper unhurriedly and rolled the cigarette between his fingers before lighting it. "If you had plenty of, uh, product, you'd have someone else selling for ya." He blew out a steady stream of smoke, then spit out a piece of tobacco that stuck to his lip. "The fact that you're doing both the butchering and selling tells me you've got a small operation going and probably need more product." He inclined his head. "Am I wrong?"

"Maybe, but who are you? You could be a copper."

"If I was, then I'd have already arrested you."

The butcher relaxed a little. "Why do you care if I have enough meat?"

"I reckon you'd probably like half a dozen fat cows. That would keep you busy for a while, wouldn't it?"

"Yeah," scoffed the butcher, "Except you don't look like a cow-cocky to me."

Eddie shrugged. "I'm not, but how hard can it be to chase a few cows into the back of a truck?"

The butcher laughed.

"Never mind, sorry to bother you, mate," Eddie said. He flicked his cigarette butt into the gutter and turned to walk away.

"Are you serious?"

Eddie stopped. "Very."

"You bring me cows and I'll give ya thirty percent," the butcher offered.

Eddie smiled, then turned and took a step closer to the butcher. "Fifty – fifty."

"I don't bloody think so."

"Alright, tell you what, sixty – forty, less expenses," Eddie offered.

"Expenses? What bloody expenses?"

"I'll need to rent a truck."

The butcher leaned forward. "You don't have a bloody truck?" he hissed. "I don't believe it." He shook his head.

Eddie looked on calmly. "Why would I use my own truck so that it could be traced back to me if someone saw what I was doing?"

The butcher conceded that the stranger had a point. He thought it over. "Righto, sixty – forty, plus expenses." The butcher thought that even if the stranger delivered, he wouldn't get half the money he expected, as there was no way for the man to know how much meat he could cut, portion, and sell. He'd put some aside and sell it on the quiet.

"I'll have something for you in two nights' time. Not tomorrow, but on Thursday," Eddie told him. "Where do I deliver?"

"I have a small paddock right behind my shed to hold the cows until they're slaughtered," the butcher informed him. "They're safe and mostly out of nosey neighbours' sight."

"Handy," said Eddie.

"Meet me here tomorrow night and I'll tell ya the address," replied the butcher.

"Tomorrow night, then." Eddie put both hands in his pockets and strolled away, whistling.

The butcher watched Eddie leave. *Be the last bloody time I see him*, he thought.

Eddie spent a good part of the day in his A56 Austin Cambridge, navigating narrow country roads on the outskirts of Oamaru. While not a farmer by any means, Eddie knew enough to understand the only way he could load cows into the back of a truck was by using a wooden-railed ramp or chute. He passed by many places which could be a good fit, but usually the farmhouse was too close. Eventually, he found the perfect location, protected by a couple of healthy macrocarpa trees and separated from the farmhouse by at least a dozen hilly corners along the winding road. The chute looked in good condition, and he suspected the cows in the paddock were to be transported soon. He hoped they'd still be there the next evening.

He returned to Oamaru to see his friend Ollie. He'd met Oliver when he was a guest of Her Majesty at Mount Eden Prison for a brief time. It was a part of his life he'd rather forget; he had hated being locked up behind bars.

Eddie sold a bogus life insurance policy to a man who died a week later when his car lost a wheel and he plunged over a steep bank in Coromandel. When the man's family tried to collect on the policy and discovered the insurance company didn't exist, they called the police. He was picked up on Karangahape Road in Auckland after signing policies for three other people, and received a two-year stint at Mount Eden for his efforts. It was where he'd met Ollie. As it turned out, Ollie proved to be a good mate, and was the reason he was now in Oamaru in the first place.

Ollie had spent a few years working as a farmhand and conveniently knew all about cows, and when Eddie discussed the job with him, and offered a ten quid incentive, he was only too happy to help. Ollie assured him that the two of them could easily load up half a dozen cows in no time at all. "Piece of cake," Ollie said with a toothless smile.

As promised, he met the butcher at the pub later, and the butcher told him they would meet at midnight, the following evening at Waiareka Junction, just out of town, and then go back to his place. The butcher explained that he wouldn't disclose his address until he saw Eddie had the cows in his truck and could confirm he wasn't being targeted by an irate farmer or the police.

This didn't bother Eddie; the previous night he'd followed the butcher home and even saw where he was hiding his money.

By using a false driver's license for identification, he paid in advance for a rental TK Bedford furniture truck. It wasn't a stock truck, but then he thought a furniture removal truck would attract less attention, and besides, he wouldn't be driving far.

He picked Ollie up around 9:00 p.m. and drove for twenty minutes or so, retracing the route he'd taken the previous day, until he arrived at the property with the cows. Eddie was relieved to see that they were still in the small paddock and hadn't been transported anywhere.

Ollie opened the rear door and Eddie slowly backed the big truck up against the chute. They kept talk to a minimum, and both kept a watchful eye for the telltale flicker of headlights to alert them of the danger of discovery.

Ollie previously explained to Eddie, "Don't shout or run at the cows. Speak softly and calmly, and they will be more manageable."

Ollie had a long stick, and with his torch and help from Eddie, he separated a small group of cows from the herd and slowly drove them into the wood-railed yard. With the gate closed, Eddie counted eight cows. *Might be too many for the butcher*, he thought. But then, they could always hire some extra help. His smile was lost in the darkness.

The cows were nervously walking up the ramp and then paused in the middle. Ollie flicked his stick gently at their hindquarters, hoping to encourage them to walk into the back of the truck.

"Hurry, mate," said Eddie. "Don't want to be here all bloody night."

"We're doin' fine," replied Ollie as he softly slapped the rump of the lead cow. She took another ponderous step, and another.

Eddie was becoming more anxious. He'd hoped the loading process would be quicker. They'd already been here for half an hour and the cows weren't in the truck yet. "C'mon, mate. Let's pick it up a bit, eh?"

It took an eternity, but Ollie wouldn't be pushed or hurried. He didn't want to excite the cows and make them unmanageable. If they were nervous, they would be stomping around in the back of the truck and kicking against the sides.

Finally, the last cow stepped into the back of the truck. It was a bit cramped, but Ollie assured him it was better this way. With the cows tightly packed, they couldn't move as much and risk hurting themselves or damaging the truck.

Eddie pulled down on the rear roller door and ran for the cab. Ollie went to follow. "Nah, stay here and cover the tyre tracks. I'll pull forward a bit."

Eddie gently eased the big truck away from the chute and onto the gravel road, and then waited as Ollie hid any signs of the truck tyre treads. When he finished, he ran back to the cab, climbed in, and before the door was closed, Eddie was already pulling away.

Resisting the temptation to speed, he drove sedately and maneuvered around corners with care. As they approached a main intersection, a car drove towards them, and Eddie and Ollie held their breath as the vehicle moved past. It wasn't the police, and they relaxed. Ollie laughed. "That was fun, eh?"

"We're not in the clear yet, mate, and just keep your eyes peeled."

"I thought you weren't going to come," said the butcher when Eddie eventually arrived at Waiareka Junction.

Eddie shrugged.

"How many did you get?"

"About eight," Eddie casually replied.

"Geezus! What am I going to do with eight bloody cows?"

"Keep your voice down and let's get out of here," Eddie warned. "I don't want to be parked here in the middle of the night and risk being caught."

"Alright, follow me," the butcher said as he looked around.

"Just drive slowly," advised Eddie.

The Bedford truck was thoroughly hosed down and cleaned before it was returned to the rental agency. The rear interior still smelled, but there was little he could do about that. The agency only partially opened the rear roller door to inspect for damage, saw none and closed the door, and Eddie's deposit was returned.

Ollie was recruited to help sell meat and stationed himself at his local pub, while Eddie went to another. They sold the meat as fast as it was cut and packaged. On Eddie's insistence, they hired another bloke for a few days to help the butcher, who was working around the clock.

The money was rolling in and exceeded Eddie's initial expectations. He was skimming off the top by charging a little more money than the price set by the butcher and pocketing the difference, and he fully expected Ollie was doing the same. The butcher was too busy cutting and packaging meat to question Eddie, especially when he delivered the daily takings and picked up the meat to take back to the pub to sell. All of them – Eddie, Ollie, the butcher, and his helper – were working their bollocks off.

Chapter Three

"That's the man I told you about," said Eileen Brewer to her son. They'd just left *Kohli's Kurry Kingdom* to celebrate her eightieth birthday and were walking to the carpark, which was also shared by the pub near the rear of the Indian restaurant.

"What man?" said Mark Brewer as he ushered his children into the back seat.

"The man whose crystal vase I broke when I collided with him as I left the post office," she replied as Marks's wife, Lee-Anne, helped her into the front seat. "He's the one at the back of the car."

Mark looked up. In the light shining from the rear entrance of the pub, he could easily see the man his mother pointed at, handing out packages to a small group of men from the boot of an Austin Cambridge. It was easy to see money was changing hands, and Mark had been around long enough to guess that whatever was being sold was probably stolen.

Mark bent down and stuck his head through the door. "And you gave him money?"

"Yes, I told you I did," she replied.

"Mum, how much did you give him?"

"It was an expensive vase. He said it had cost him five pounds."

"Five…!" He shook his head. "Mum, you were conned. Tricked." Mark straightened and looked across the carpark for a moment before taking a step closer to get a better look at the man. His hat kept his face in the darkness, and Mark couldn't see much, but he saw the car's registration plate and memorized the number.

From the car, he heard the kids begin to grizzle.

"Mark, it's late and we need to get the kids in bed," his wife reminded him.

Mark returned to his car and climbed inside. "How do you know that's the man? It's dark."

"Same clothes, and the way he wears his hat, that angle. I'm sure it's him."

"And you gave him *five pounds?*" he asked again in growing anger.

"Yes, but why do you say he tricked me? I knocked into him and broke the vase; I saw the pieces…"

Eddie Ricketts knew he would have to leave Oamaru soon. He'd been in this town long enough, and the longer he stayed, the higher was the risk of being caught.

At the rate they were selling meat, they'd run out within the next three days, and already the butcher was suggesting that they should hit another farm. That made Eddie nervous; he had no intention of rustling more cattle. However, to keep the butcher from suspecting he was planning to leave, he enthusiastically agreed. Little did the butcher know that Eddie intended to steal all *his* takings before he departed.

At the end of each day, Eddie and the butcher would count their earnings and divide the money as agreed. Afterwards, when Eddie returned to the boarding house where he lived, the butcher would extract a wooden box from a big freezer, put the bundle of money in a plastic bag, and then place the bag in the box before returning it to the freezer.

Eddie calculated that the butcher had amassed about a hundred quid, give or take, and that was a substantial amount of money. When the butcher discovered his money was missing, he wouldn't be able to go to the police, and if he decided to look for Eddie himself, he'd most likely go north. When they talked, Eddie had dropped hints that when this job was over, he'd return to Wellington, when in fact he was planning to head south to Invercargill.

The evening after his mother's birthday dinner, Mark Brewer returned alone to the same parking lot at the rear of the pub and went inside to have a beer. He waited to see if the man his mother identified would appear; he was going to try to find out what was he selling. He had a suspicion, but first he needed to confirm it. Mark was well on the way into his second handle when the stranger showed up. It didn't take long before Mark's guess was confirmed. He learned that the man was selling meat, and was almost certain it was stolen.

Mark spent the next morning on the phone. As a stock agent, he knew most farmers in the area, and it didn't take long to learn that eight cows had been taken from Davidson's farm just over a week ago. Mr. Davidson was enraged when Mark telephoned him, and wanted to grab his rifle, go to the pub, and shoot the bastard. After a short while, he calmed down, and Mark arranged to visit him later that afternoon for a chat.

"What did the police say?" Mark asked.
"They're looking into it, but typically, not a bloody thing so far," Mr. Davidson exclaimed with a measure of disgust.

Mark was silent a moment. "That bloke also conned my mum out of five pounds."

Mr. Davidson shook his head. "The lousy bastard."

Mark Brewer sat with Mr. Davidson and his three boys around their kitchen table as they discussed various options of catching and punishing the man. None were viable, although castrating him seemed tempting until Mark reminded them of the bloody mess it would make.

Mr. Davidson's three sons were all adults, and like their father, were frothing at the bit to get their hands on the crook.

"You know he can't be acting alone, as someone is butchering the meat and others are selling," Mark suggested. "Catching just one of them won't stop it from happening again."

The eldest son, Adam, spoke up. "Why don't we watch the pub and follow him, find out where he goes? He'd have to go somewhere to pick up the meat, wouldn't he?" He looked at his two younger brothers, who nodded in support.

"You're on to something there," Mark chipped in. "I want you to be able to recover the cost of your cows. If we go to the police, you'd have two chances of getting any money back, *slim* and *none*, especially if he's also stolen from others and they put in a claim as well."

Mr. Davidson nodded in agreement. "Yep, let's find out who's behind this rustling gang. But what then? What do we do when we know who the others are?"

Mark scooted his chair closer to the table. "I've got an idea."

"Does it involve your brother-in-law?" asked Mr. Davidson.

Chapter Four

Eddie informed the butcher that Ollie had injured himself and couldn't assist with rustling cows in two days' time. The butcher, keen as ever, volunteered to fill that role, and Eddie reluctantly agreed. He explained to the butcher that the farm he'd selected was on the other side of Oamaru, quite some distance from the butcher's property.

"I'm not bloody driving south to pick you up and then up north into Canterbury. We'll need to meet somewhere," Eddie told him. "Anyway, having a spare vehicle just in case isn't a bad idea, and if we run into a spot of bother, we can always ditch the truck."

The butcher, who Eddie thought was a little slow, finally nodded in agreement. "Alright, makes sense."

The two men were finalizing plans to heist their next herd of cows and stood talking in the large shed the butcher used to cut up meat. Unknown to them both, an old Ford Prefect sat parked alongside the road, a short distance from the butcher's property. Inside the vehicle, Adam Davidson and his younger brother Stephen were waiting. They'd followed the Austin Cambridge from the pub and believed this was the location where the cows were butchered once they saw the large shed door slide open, revealing a large butcher's wooden chopping block and an old bandsaw.

"Soon as I leave with the rental truck, I'll telephone you and you can meet me in Pukeuri, where state highway one meets highway eighty-three."

You got it?" Eddie asked the butcher. "We should arrive about the same time."

"Yeah, yeah, I know. You've already told me three times," said the butcher.

"Good, I'm just making sure, that's all."

At about the time when the butcher was supposed to arrive at the meeting place, Eddie figured he'd be helping himself to the butcher's stash of money. He just needed the man away from his house. By the time the butcher returned home, Eddie would already have driven many miles away from Oamaru and would be safely on his way southwards. Eddie was pleased; his trip to Oamaru had been very profitable.

The Davidson boys reported their findings to their father, who in turn called Mark Brewer on the telephone. "Is as I thought. We now got the butcher," said Mark happily after hearing from Mr. Davidson.

"When do we make our move?" asked the older man.

"The day after next. I can't do it tomorrow, as I have a stock sale in Timaru," Mark replied. "But make sure your boys are ready. We can only do this if there is enough of us, and your lads are big boys. That will intimidate them," replied Mark.

Mr. Davidson laughed. "I'm sure my boys will."

Eddie Ricketts phoned the butcher from a telephone box about a five-minute drive from his house. He told him he had the rental truck and would meet him at their pre-arranged location in approximately forty minutes.

Eddie got out of the telephone box and walked down the street.

Standing behind a tree, he waited for the butcher to drive past in his van. Within a couple of minutes, the van rattled past, trailing a cloud of blue smoke.

Earlier, Eddie had slipped unseen from the boarding house with his suitcase, without paying the money he owed for accommodation. He didn't feel any remorse or guilt, and genuinely believed that if the couple who operated the boarding house were stupid enough not to demand an upfront payment, they deserved what they got.

He arrived at the darkened home of the butcher and reversed into the driveway, backing up to the sliding door of the large shed. Without fear or worry, he stepped from the car, opened the boot, extracted a large set of bolt-cutters, and proceeded to cut the padlock on the shed door. He wasn't concerned about being seen. The nearest neighbours were at least two hundred yards away, and separated by a hedge of poplar trees, and he knew the butcher wouldn't be back for about two hours.

He slid the door open, flicked on the light switch, and headed towards a large freezer. Half a side of beef hung forlornly from a hook – the last of their meat. He slapped the beef with his hand as he walked past. "Cheers. Better you than me," he said with a grin.

With confidence, he lifted the freezer lid, rummaged inside, and found the treasured wooden box where the butcher kept his takings. He paused and looked over his shoulder, down towards the street as he heard an approaching car. The vehicle spluttered past the house and continued down the road. Relieved, Eddie opened the box and saw a plastic bag containing three large wads of rolled-up notes held together by rubber bands. He whistled. It was more than he expected.

He grabbed the bag, tossed the empty box back into the freezer, and returned to his car, leaving the bag on the front seat. He would hide the money later, when safely away.

His car began to roll down the driveway when suddenly, headlight beams swung across the road, and a full-size Land Rover bounced up the driveway and slid to a stop, blocking him. The blinding headlights remained on. Eddie was puzzled; the butcher drove a Bedford van, and he didn't know anyone with a Land Rover. He raised his arm to shield his eyes from the glare and decided to investigate. Whoever this was wanted the butcher, and he could easily explain his presence here. He climbed from his car as he heard the Land Rover's four doors closing.

"G'day. The butcher isn't here. Don't know where he is," said Eddie into the brilliance of full beam headlights.

Another car pulled up and parked on the road. He couldn't see anything, but again heard a car door slam.

"We've been looking for you," said a voice from a man unseen.

Someone walked past Eddie towards the shed. Eddie turned to look to see who it was. He didn't recognize him, but it was a big bloke who looked like a rugby player.

"Geezus, it stinks!" yelled the rugby player as he peered into the shed. "There's half a side hanging in here. Only the one, though."

"Ya bloody bastard," snapped Mr. Davidson and took an aggressive step forward.

Eddie raised his hands. "Fellas, I don't know what this is all about. I came here to get some money the butcher owes me, that's all. I don't know what he's done, but I 'aint part of it. Honest!"

"You stole from these men," said Mark Brewer, stepping closer. "Cattle rustling doesn't go down well here. You–"

"You got the wrong bloke," Eddie appealed, feeling the first stirrings of real concern. He was scared.

"We saw you in the pub. We saw you selling meat you rustled, so don't lie," Mark replied angrily.

Adam Davidson looked inside the Austin Cambridge. Eddie had left his door open and lit by the Land Rover's headlights, Adam saw the plastic bag on the seat. "Dad, look what I found!"

"Bastard!" spat Mr. Davidson when Adam handed him the bundle of cash.

Eddie was frantically thinking of a way to escape. He looked right and left, panicking, and suddenly felt his arms grabbed from either side.

Epilogue

Eddie Ricketts couldn't move. He was bound tightly to the beef carcass that hung inside the butcher's shed. The men who'd apprehended him had searched through his car and found his stash of money – and these men also had the butcher's plastic bag of cash, which really pissed him off. They'd blindfolded him and tied him up, and he honestly believed they were going to maim or even possibly kill him. He'd overheard one of the men talking about castration. There was nothing he could do. He felt urine run down his legs.

He tensed as he heard footfalls approaching.

"You robbed my mother of five pounds, and God knows how many other people you have stolen from," said Mark. "We are taking all the money we found here tonight and will try to return it to the rightful owners."

"Ya lousy bastard!" said Mr. Davidson.

Eddie heard them walk away and shut the door to the shed. He jiggled and tried to pull his hands and feet free, but that hurt and only seemed to make it worse. The cow carcass was cold and clammy.

"Here's the five pounds that bastard took from your mum," said Mr. Davidson as he handed a note from the butcher's wad over to Mark. He reached into his pocket, took out his wallet, and extracted another five-pound note. "And this is also for her, my birthday present. Tell her that I'm paying for her to have her hair done." He stood beside his Land Rover; his sons were already inside. He lifted the bag of money. "This won't cover my loss, but it'll help." He looked back to the shed. "Bastard!" he shouted.

"Oh, thank you, Mr. Davidson. She'll be thrilled. She was so disappointed she couldn't have her hair done for her birthday dinner." Mark smiled. "I'll give her the money tomorrow."

"Are you going to make that call?" Mr. Davidson asked.

"Yep, soon as I find a phone box," Mark affirmed.

"Thank you for all you've done. We'll talk next week. I have a few head I need to sell," said Mr. Davidson as he climbed into his Land Rover.

Mark walked to his car and heard the muffled yell, "Bastard!" come from inside the Land Rover. He laughed.

Mark drove back towards Oamaru and stopped at the first telephone box he saw. He coined the money and dialed the number he knew by heart. Someone answered after the third ring.

"Hello?"

He pressed the 'A' button and heard the coin drop. "Sarge, it's me."

"Brewski, how are ya?" replied Mark's brother-in-law, using his nickname.

"Am great. You know that report about the eight cattle rustled last week from the Davidson farm?"

"Yeah, what of it?" The tone of the voice changed.

"I think you oughta take a look at seventeen Cook Street. You'll find someone hanging around who may be able to assist you with this enquiry, and a few others besides."

"Cook Street, eh? Why are you involved?"

"I'll tell you over a beer, but you better send someone quick. I believe another accomplice will be returning soon."

"Alrighty, will do. And this *is* the rustler…?"

"At the butcher's home," Mark confirmed.

"The bastards!" said his brother-in-law before hanging up.

BROWN SHOES

Wellington, 1975

There was a knock at the door. It wasn't a casual friendly knock of a neighbour or the timid knock of a child; it was a distinctive, authoritative knock that required immediate consideration.

At the intrusion, Arthur Potts looked up from his newspaper and grunted. He knew about door knocks, he'd heard a lifetime of them, and many more than he ever cared to remember. Door knocks were a nuisance and always inconvenient, just as they were now, and no one could convince him otherwise.

With a heavy sigh, he quickly folded the newspaper he was reading and without regard, casually tossed it onto the table that sat beside his chair. The paper unexpectedly fell to the floor. A look of bewilderment crossed his face and he shook his head slightly as he peered over the side of the chair to look. *Odd. Who moved the lamp-table*, he wondered?

He reached up, removed his reading glasses, and from the right pocket of his jacket extracted a scarred and worn spectacle case. With knurled, arthritic hands and a slight tremor, he fumbled for a moment, opened the cover and carefully nestled his glasses into the lens cleaning cloth. With a flick, the lid snapped shut and he replaced the case precisely where it belonged, back into the right, hip pocket of his jacket.

Still perplexed by the peculiarity of the missing lamp, he reached for his other glasses, the ones with the silver, wire frames that Elizabeth chose for him. He'd put them down when he'd arrived earlier with the newspaper, and placed them on the round table beside him as he always did, but the table had gone. *Where was it*, he thought? His brow furrowed as he tried to contemplate the mystery. It just didn't make sense.

There it was again, the incessant knock. "People are in such a hurry these days," he mumbled. He placed both hands on the armrests, slowly eased upright and stood on creaky, senescent legs.

Curious as to where the table and his glasses had disappeared to, he looked again, but they weren't to be seen. A floor lamp with a small round table affixed and a rose-coloured shade with tassels should have stood sentinel at his armrest. Now there was nothing but a forgotten children's toy, a small plastic block of some sort where the lamp should've sat. He looked elsewhere. At a different place in the room, he saw a shiny, black, awful - looking thing with a glass top that sat rudely on the floor. "Modern furniture; no character," he grizzled. Again, he twisted around and searched for his glasses and wondered where they'd gone.

For the briefest moment, he doubted himself, and beginning with his trousers, gave each pocket a pat, working his way upwards until he was satisfied he didn't have them.

"Lizzie, love, get the damn door can you, I can't find my glasses!" he yelled.

He paused and listened but heard no reply. *Where'd she go?*

Puzzled, he scratched his chin, the coarse stubble reminding him he'd forgotten to shave this morning.

"Mr. Potts!"

He heard the muted unrecognizable voice of the caller.

Automatically he reached with both hands and ensured his tie was tight and centred. With a practised forefinger, he pressed the knot and straightened his jacket, before taking an uncertain step and retrieved his walking stick that still lay propped against the back of the chair. No sign of his glasses, though.

Where was Elizabeth? *She should be here.* His mouth twitched at the beginning of a smile as he realised she must be shopping with the kids. That's why the house is so quiet. Dear Elizabeth, she really did look after him.

The thought of her shopping for groceries made him realise he was hungry. He couldn't remember when he last ate. "Wednesday, Wednesday," he muttered. Ah yes, a roast. Elizabeth always cooked a roast on Wednesdays. Other than Saturdays, Wednesday was his favourite day of the week. The newspaper was always thick and full of news, the Situations Vacant section had plenty of jobs and then there were the ads, lots of useful things for sale.

Knock, knock, knock.

There it was again, that confounded knock.

"Mr Potts, we know you're inside!" came the unknown male voice.

"Cheeky sod," replied Arthur quietly, more to himself than anyone.

"Hold your horses, coming," he said, but it came out as a croak.

He cleared his throat and tried again. "Hold your horses!"

He took an uncertain step, then stopped. A brief look of confusion passed across his craggy face. With his right hand, he scratched his head and dislodged a few wispy white hairs that now stood awkwardly on end.

'Mr. Potts, answer the door!"

"Coming." His voice little more than a whisper.

He shuffled forwards, his shiny, brown leather shoes silent on the carpet now sounded loud on the pinewood floor as he turned from the living room into the hallway. He took another two steps, and from a force of habit slid his right foot near the wall and pressed down. The floorboard creaked, just as it always did. He grinned.

From outside, someone rattled the door handle.

"Hey!" shouted Arthur Potts, indignant at the rudeness of the caller. He hacked at the exertion and his eyes watered. He pulled a handkerchief from his trousers and wiped his mouth and eyes and returned it from where it came.

The rattling stopped. At least he'd had the presence of mind to lock the door when he came home. *Can't trust people these days*, he mused.

With his foot still on the floorboard, he turned to his left and stared open-mouthed where the photograph of he and Elizabeth standing arm-in-arm on a platform at Wellington Railway Station should have been. Momentarily confused, he blinked, and his eyes narrowed as he squinted at the gaudy painting of a misshapen bird that hung grotesquely in its place. *Have to find my glasses*, he reaffirmed to himself as he glared vacantly at the blurry image, that glorious day with her so vivid in memory.

The knocking persisted, and Arthur turned from the painting and stared forlornly at the door. He swallowed, and for a fleeting instance, felt doubt and an overwhelming sadness that had no meaning. The hammering on the door continued and with his walking stick leading the way, slowly advanced down the hall towards the door.

Each step took an age, and with it, Arthur felt increasingly alone. He stopped once and looked behind, in case Elizabeth returned home through the back, kitchen door, but the house was still empty. She'd be home soon, he knew.

The knocking and knob jiggling stopped. Whoever was outside must have heard him as he shuffled down the hall. "Good, let the impatient sod wait a bit longer" he griped.

He reached for the familiar handle, twisted the lock, took a half step back and swung the door open.

The inquisitive and fresh youthful face of a constable stood staring. Behind him on a lower step, two strange women gaped, one looking very angry and the other teary-eyed and clutching a frilly hanky.

"Dad, we've been looking for you everywhere!" exclaimed the teary one.

Dad? He inclined his head in bafflement.

The policeman extended his hand, "C'mon Mr. Potts."

He turned from the policeman and looked at the two unfamiliar women curiously. If he had his glasses he could see them better.

The angry woman looked irritated and stood with her arms folded.

"It's time to take you home, Dad," said the woman with the hanky.

"And let this be the last time he does this," admonished the angry one.

"I apologise, we'll see to it that he doesn't do it again, don't worry."

The old man didn't understand what the fuss was about and turned to each face in question.

The policeman took his walking stick and gently grasped his elbow to help him across the threshold.

His bottom lip quivered and his pale grey eyes stared blankly, not comprehending. "My newspaper, and, and my glasses, I can't find my glasses," he uttered almost apologetically, his voice cracking. He twisted his head to look back inside. "Elizabeth will be home soon, she's shopping with the kids, she won't know where I've gone."

The woman with the hanky reached past the constable and held something in her hand. "Here are your glasses, dad. It's time to come home."

"But Elizabeth … she'll wonder where I am," he appealed as he put on his spectacles.

"Mum's been dead for twenty years," she said softly.

He turned to look at her in puzzlement, then his eyes welled and he lowered his head in embarrassment to blink at the ground.

"Can I go inside and get his newspaper?" asked the lady with the hanky. "He loves his paper."

The other woman's expression softened. She smiled ruefully and nodded.

"C'mon Mr. Potts, let's get you home," said the policeman.

216

.